UNDERLIFE

Robert Finn

ISBN 9781905005697

Clipper spent a lot of time on the tube. It had a buzz he liked. And anything you could want was down there. Hurried people with too much money. Anonymity and good exit routes. Hot girls you'd never normally set eyes on – and they were stuck there for five minutes waiting for a train – no excuse for not talking to you. Sometimes Clipper would even help bewildered tourists. Of course if he was a little drunk or a little high, his help tended to really mess up their travel plans, but by and large he meant it well. Though lately he was cutting back on that – the getting high, as well as the freelance tourist advice. Gary had never let him get away with it anyway and somehow doing what Gary wanted seemed even more important now that he was gone.

So now Clipper's watchword was 'professionalism'. Though if he did happen to be a little high he'd try to avoid actually saying it out loud; all those syllables tended to trip your tongue up.

The problem was that he was by himself now and that messed everything up. For a start it meant he was having to make all his own plans, and that required concentration. Which was a problem. Whatever he tried, he just couldn't seem to motivate himself properly. His concentration slipped away from him the whole time and he found himself drifting, wasting time. And that was dangerous. It meant it was only a matter of time before he screwed up and got caught.

It was more than that too. When Gary disappeared, it didn't just leave a gap that needed to be filled, it changed things. Maybe for good.

If Clipper had had another way of earning a living he'd have been giving it some careful consideration at this point.

Today he was hanging round the Jubilee line, sort of goofing off despite his best intentions. Riding from Bond Street – where the best-looking shop assistants in the world worked – out to Canary Wharf – where you'd get these career girls in their suits, with their amazing hair that looked so natural because they'd spent a mint getting it that way. Great looking and they were all brokers or traders or bankers – if you could have girl bankers.

Brainy and in charge. He always liked that. And he always wished he'd been able to get somewhere with one of them. It was probably as much to see what their lives looked like as anything. He imagined they all lived in loft apartments – wood floors and little twinkly halogen lights – with gyms in the basement. And their boyfriends were Swiss ski instructors or else they were really old blokes with big, big amounts of cash – like from owning oil tankers or some copper mines. And it didn't matter that the blokes were like sixty or something because that was exactly the point about having stacks of cash.

Those thoughts had been vaguely in the back of his mind as he'd been eyeing up this one girl, trying not to let her notice he was paying attention. He was glancing at her, and letting his imagination wander, when really he knew he should have been working on the next grab.

They were outside, above ground, in what the signs called a 'plaza' by the entrance to Canary Wharf tube. A needling wind was skipping round Clipper's ankles, making him wish he'd brought that big old gangsta puffa jacket of his. Nearby the girl was talking on the phone, oblivious to him, tucking hair the colour of maple syrup behind her delicate ear and cutting up rough in what he thought was probably German. And yet she wasn't German because every now and then she'd swear or say 'get used to it' in English, only with an American accent. How hot was that? She was tearing a strip off some bloke in German and then dissing him in English, like rubbing his nose in how it wasn't even her first language that she was clobbering him in.

He reckoned she might be Californian. As he liked to remind people, he'd lived there for a few years himself – though he tended not to get very specific, because the truth was he'd been at high-school there for a few years and that probably didn't sound as impressive as whatever story people might come up with for themselves if he kept fairly quiet about the details. Relocating out there to be with his dad and then pulling up roots and coming back again had badly messed with his half-hearted attempts to get an education – not to mention how it had mongrelised the slang he used – but it had also left him with just enough of an accent, and maybe a bit of added mystery, so he wasn't complaining.

The girl had finished her first call and was dialling another. She took a deep breath before putting the phone to her ear and he could tell it wasn't a conversation she was looking forward to.

He really should get going, but there was something about this girl, besides her looks – and he found himself unable to look away. He watched her getting her nerve up before speaking and he couldn't help feel a bit sorry for whatever she was going through.

For a moment he thought about nicking her phone, a Blackberry (natch), but he couldn't get very excited about the idea, even if there'd been an easy way to make it happen.

Without thinking, he stepped in a little closer to her, careful to keep his eyes up ahead like he didn't see her. He was sort of hoping to catch a hint of whatever perfume she was wearing. He wasn't, you know, a pervert or anything – it was just that these girls always smelled amazing.

Afterwards, if he was looking back on that day and trying to choose a particular moment, he'd have to say that right then, as he stepped forwards, was probably when things started to unravel. It was about the last thing to happen that day that really made any sort of sense. Everything after that point was like a really unpleasant episode from someone else's life spliced into his, not to mention that most of it took place in fast-forward. Even the bits that weren't a speeded-up nightmare were still like something out of a dream, though at least it was one of his own.

The girl had made her difficult call. Clipper had stuck around, trying not to look conspicuous, but still watching her face, somehow captivated. Then she'd hung up, and so softly you'd hardly notice, she'd begun to cry. From then on, that whole day just rocketed past him, one insane event after another, all seemingly unstoppable.

The girl had begun to cry and it had hurt him – it had physically hurt him – watching her face. A pain just under his ribs, like something sharp was pressing into a soft part of him, had forced him into motion. One minute he was detached, keeping out of her eye line, just a spectator; the next he was moving quickly forwards, asking gently, "Are you OK?" He could hear the compassion in his voice and knew that he meant it – though he had no explanation for it. But then it didn't seem to need explaining. She was upset; he wanted to help. It didn't require any more thought than if she'd stumbled and he'd caught her.

He was confused at his own behaviour and it seemed to have caught her off guard too. She should have glared at him, because he was a stranger intruding on a private moment, or at least she should have lied like normal people do and said, "I'm fine." But instead she told him exactly why she was crying.

And then they'd just talked.

It had been unlike any conversation he'd ever had. She said her name and he told her his: his real name. And it was... perfect.

Really, it was just about too good to be true. Of course as soon as he thought that, the world slid back into focus around him and he realised what he'd just told her – said right out, to a total stranger – and he felt panic. A panic that took on a different dimension when, out of the corner of his eye, he clocked a black shape moving towards him. Something about it held his attention. He looked round and was instantly annoyed with himself. This was what happened when you let your mind wander away from the business in hand.

The shape he'd seen was a black car, some sort of expensive 4x4, and it had stopped at the top of the steps behind him. It was probably the way the car had pulled up that had caught his eye. You couldn't park there – not even for a minute. He didn't know what it meant, but it sparked a little flash of adrenaline inside him.

The car – which was maybe an X5, that slick BMW SUV – spat out a couple of fast-moving geezers in black, who were dressed like coppers, but sort of tougher. Some sort of tactical group maybe.

His rising sense of anxiety over the arrival of a police car was starting to push away the acute shame he felt after his chat with the girl. He'd told her... well, he'd blurted out all sorts of things and he felt embarrassed and kind of exposed now. He'd made an idiot of himself and he just wanted to get away from her before she could point that fact out. The sense that the cops were bearing down on him magnified his agitation until he could hardly hold still. He needed to move. "Gotta go," he said to her, even as he skipped away.

He did what he called his 'fade'. He matched speed with a couple of secretaries who were click-clacking past, and shifted from his usual walk, which was kind of a chin-forwards swagger, to more of a rapid shuffle – what he thought of as his office-boy walk. Hassled and downtrodden. And today he was in the right clothes to pull it off. A month back he'd got a dark blue suit from Moss Bros – forty quid because it had glue or something on one of the trouser legs and a snag on the right lapel. He'd added a white shirt and a silver tie he'd stolen from Next: so freaked to be in there that he'd pocketed it on instinct. Looking at the other shoppers, he'd had a sudden glimpse of what his life could be like if he was a trainee estate agent or, you know, maybe working in credit control for a car leasing firm or something, and he'd bolted, forgetting his original plan to actually pay for the thing. Black shoes, which were bashed to bits, and his hair like he usually had it. Short all round with a sort of teased mop on top. It wasn't an office haircut, but then he was always seeing these junior types dressed just like that: creased-up office clothes and mad club hairstyles. Suits that looked like they slept in them. Maybe when you had a crap job on crap pay you got to have your hair how you wanted it.

Clipper felt better for being on the move. He was now angling towards the archway at the top of the escalator, the one that led down into the tube station, and thinking it was time to get out of the cold. The girl was forgotten – or at any rate he was working on it – and there was no denying that it was, as his granddad used to say, perishin' outside. He'd leave the coppers to their business.

But he risked a glance in their direction anyway, because he had a thing for any sort of cool-sounding elite police stuff, ever since he was a kid. They seemed to be heading in the same direction he was. So he began to turn away, so as not to put himself in their sights.

Speaking of which, he was hoping they'd be carrying guns. But they weren't. They'd got everything else though. The whole outfit screamed weapons training. Altberg Defender boots, ballistic flak tunics, lots of webbing and everything in black. The bulky flak tunics sort of ended at the shoulder, like a cap-sleeve t-shirt. If you happened to have ripped deltoids – which these guys did, you could see them bunching under their tight nylon sleeves – then you weren't going to have any problems looking serious in that get-up. He'd hoped for SWAT-style helmets, but they had on tight knitted caps instead. Very SAS. He took in as many of these details as he could, thinking how he'd google it all later. Both men were white and Clipper had more stubble on his chin than either of them had on what he could see of their heads. SO19 maybe? The Met's Armed Response group. Or maybe something lower profile?

Clipper was more than a little bit torn now. Part of him, the part he was doing his best to ignore, wanted to rush back to the girl, to ask her, "What just happened between us?" But he wasn't planning to act on that particular impulse. The rest of his brain was trying to decide how to react to these coppers. If there was any chance that they could be after him, or if the area was about to be sealed off, he needed to scarper. But these blokes had to be some sort of anti-terrorism outfit, which let him off the hook, didn't it? Besides which he just ate up that stuff. He wanted to know why they were here, what they were planning to do. Maybe something was going on.

Gary would have dragged him away, of course – he was all for the low-key, better part of valour stuff – but Gary was gone. And Clipper thought he'd like to get a *slightly* better look at what they were up to. With that in mind, he peeled off from the city gent he was now following, and began to loop slowly around so that the SWAT-looking guys could lead the way. If he got behind them instead of letting them bear down on him, he'd feel a lot happier about sticking around.

While he split off to the side, pretending he wanted to take a quick look at the quayside, he watched them out of the corner of his eye. They didn't talk, didn't use their radios, didn't even glance towards each other, but they moved together in a way that made Clipper *yearn* to be part of some organisation like that. Watching them walk, it was like a Tarantino thing, only they weren't in slow motion.

It reminded him of a daydream he had where he was recruited as an undercover member of some tactical unit like that. In the daydream they'd been watching him for a while, could see he was a bright guy and they were prepared to clean his record if he'd come and work for them… undercover. Which he didn't consider completely farfetched. Clipper knew what was what and boxed a little and liked to think he was in shape; all he'd need to get him ready for some special forces job was a little specialist training. Mind you, these lads in front of him looked like they'd had more than a *little* training. They were just about the toughest pair he'd ever seen. Try as he might, he couldn't see himself getting in their way for a second. Couldn't picture it.

Fascinated, he let them get on the down escalator, hung back as a stream of ordinary punters stepped on behind them and then, some distance back, he followed them down into the cavern of the station and the relative warmth below.

Every day, Clipper's first job was always to boost a travelcard and he had one in his pocket right now, but the spook-force guys were stalled up ahead, flashing badges and saying something to the trog on the ticket barriers ('trog' was what Gary called the underground staff) so Clipper busied himself with a ticket machine for a minute to make sure he didn't end up ahead of them again.

The transport bloke was looking very unhappy to see them, like they'd just offered to demonstrate some of their excellent specialist training on him. Right away the man was sweating. He was shaking his head and holding up his hands too, which they obviously didn't care for. Then one of the badge-flashing coppers took a step towards him. Simultaneously his partner laid a finger on his arm, halting him, but the transport bloke looked like he was about to lose some sphincter control. He fumbled a gate open for them and they pushed through leaving the trog standing there, looking all around for guidance, clearly not sure what he was supposed to do next.

Whatever this was about, Clipper was lapping it up. It was a treat to see a trog sweating for a change. They were always recognising him, making his life difficult, throwing their weight around. Now one of them was on the receiving end for once. *Yeah*, thought Clipper, looking at the rattled transport bloke and revelling in the way he'd been brushed aside, *back off*.

Moving through the gates and onto the escalator, leaving the flustered trog behind, Clipper lost sight of the cops for a minute. Maybe they'd double-timed it on ahead. Clipper thought about running to catch up, but he knew Gary would have had a fit at the thought if he'd been there. Sprinting after coppers being perhaps the stupidest idea ever. The whole point of working the underground was that it made you anonymous, impossible to remember, one of ten million faceless faces. What you didn't do – what you didn't *ever* do – was stand out. Because not only did it mess up whatever angle you were working at that moment, it risked messing up the next one and so on down the line. Pretty soon they'd be spotting your face on CCTV and passing out your photo and everyone knew what happened next. And in Gary's case what had happened next was prison. This was before Clipper had met him and it had only been an eighteen month sentence, which never sounded that bad to Clipper, but he tended to keep his mouth shut on that point on account of how Gary knew his real name was Matthew and he had a mum living in Bromley who liked to make him beans on toast on the rare occasions he dropped in and he'd never been 'inside' or even in a cell overnight and so any view he might have on prison would be based on sitting in a nice cosy flat eating his tea and watching it on telly.

Clipper tried to cut off that line of thought because the truth was that he was thinking about Gary the whole time. He missed him. Not only did Gary keep him out of trouble, and dispense these little gems of wisdom the whole time, but he was the one who made the whole thing fun. Without him it wasn't an adventure any more; it was just stealing things and trying not to get caught.

Gary, who'd read a lot of books – especially inside – was always making genius stuff up, like how he and Clipper were the Marxist Vanguard. Clipper never really knew what that meant, but Gary would quote the phrase 'all property is theft', which Clipper really liked, and it had become like a catchphrase for them both.

Sometimes when Clipper thought about Gary's disappearance, an unwelcome thought crept into his head; he worried that Gary had disappeared on purpose.

The first few times Gary had gone on errands for the mysterious Warren, and left Clipper to fend for himself, it had seemed like the beginning of the end. Whatever Warren had Gary doing, it was obviously a lot more fun than dipping for wallets and phones and such on the tube. Clipper had the sense that Gary was moving up in the world without him, like some sort of underworld promotion that Clipper had been passed over for.

That hadn't lasted long though. After the third job – and Gary would never say what the jobs actually involved – his mood had changed and it no longer seemed like Gary was off having fun. He was very subdued and he said even less about what he did for Warren, but Clipper got the distinct impression it wasn't for the fainthearted.

Clipper had seen Warren a few times, always from a distance. And the last time had also been the last time he'd seen Gary.

He and Gary had gone to a club that was supposedly part-owned by Warren. It really wasn't Gary's scene, though Clipper was quite into it, being a few years younger and a little less awkward when it came to being around loud music and girls dancing.

Gary had left Clipper talking to a couple of nurses from Hatfield and gone back behind the bar with a flunky who'd come to fetch him, saying that Warren was ready to see him now. Clipper kept up a bit of patter with the nurses, doing his best not to get distracted, but all the time he was watching out for any glimpse of Gary returning.

Because Clipper was with Gary, and Gary was with Warren, the bar was comping their drinks. So when Clipper finally did get a glimpse of Gary an hour or so later, it was after several more bottles of very tasty imported beer and he was no longer at his most lucid – over-refreshed was how he liked to think of it. The nurses were packing up, Clipper having got a little too Mr Grabby with one of them, when he saw Gary at the back of the club near one of the exits. Gary was nodding to an imposing looking bloke with a scarred face who stood nearby. Gary looked like he was trying to reassure him he was on the case. Clipper was pretty sure it was the same man he'd glimpsed before, and there was clearly a boss/employee vibe involved, so it had to be Warren. Clipper tried to get a proper look at the man, but the club lighting didn't help with that. Warren was dressed pretty sharply, though he wore some sort of tight skull-cap. It was difficult to tell whether it was the latest Hollywood fad or some religious thing. Despite looking pretty weird, it also looked sort of natural too. So much so that Clipper wondered about getting one too.

Gary had given a final nod, this one meaning goodbye, and strode away towards one of the exits without even a glance towards Clipper. Then out of nowhere, a Slavic looking guy was stepping up behind Warren and smacking him across the back of the head with an empty beer bottle.

Fragments of green glass sprayed across the nearest table, hitting some girl in the face, and triggering a scream that Clipper could hear from across the room. It cut through the pounding of a Sasha remix like a gunshot at a funeral.

Warren didn't go down though, he twisted round to place one hand over the spot where the bottle had hit, and then everything went peculiar.

What Clipper thought he saw was the Slavic guy ramming the shattered bottle in a twisting motion towards Warren's throat and the glass teeth grinding themselves to pieces all by themselves. For an eerie second he appeared to be holding the bottle steady a foot or so from Warren's throat. But at the same time, it seemed like he was leaning into it. It wasn't an image that made a lot of sense.

Then Warren straightened and pushed out with his palm, like an open-hand punch, which to Clipper never seemed to connect, but the Slavic guy went down with a snap, almost like a convulsion, as though he'd been bitten by the world's deadliest snake.

That done, Warren snatched a fresh cloth from the bar, pressed it to his bleeding head and leaned across to say something in the ear of a bouncer who'd rushed over. He didn't appear to be bothered by the damage done to his scalp or to notice the blood running out from under his skull-cap and down the back of his neck. A moment later, two other bouncers were carrying the fallen man into a back room and Warren was staring at the girl with the cut face, coldly assessing her, while one of the bar girls tried to stop her crying.

Gary was nowhere to be seen. Numb – both with shock and effects of the beer – Clipper did his best to get out of there quickly. He hunted up and down the street without success, and finally caught up with Gary at a cab place about five minutes later. For a moment he couldn't think what to say.

"Who is he?" he asked in the end.

Gary looked distracted, wrapped up in his own weary thoughts, and only half aware of Clipper standing there. "They're all..." he said and tapered off. His eyes weren't even focussed on Clipper. They were set on the middle-distance, where presumably he could play out and review whatever thoughts were bothering him.

A cab pulled up at the kerb and the dispatcher tapped on the scratched window, caught Gary's eye, and pointed to it. In something of a daze, Gary wandered towards the idling vehicle.

"Gary?" Clipper said sharply, trying to get his attention.

Gary turned to look at him, finally fixing on his face. "You can't hurt them," he said absently and then he was getting into a cab, leaving Clipper standing on the pavement in a shiny shirt that was glued to his back with sweat that got colder every second and did nothing to dispel the feeling that something good had ended.

And that was the last time Clipper had seen Gary. No one knew where he'd gone, but a lot people had suggested it was somewhere unpleasant and permanent. Clipper's guts knotted at the thought. But at the same time he somehow didn't like the idea that Gary was alive and well any better – that maybe he'd made a few bob on that last job for Warren and then decided he was better off without Clipper, that he didn't need him any more. It was a toss-up as to which idea upset him more.

Now, riding down on the escalator, Clipper tried for the millionth time to stop thinking about Gary and what had happened to him. He tried to focus on the present as he stepped off onto the platform, which at Canary Wharf was a great concrete cathedral of hollowed-out space. He looked around, realising with a little jolt that he couldn't see the spook-force coppers anywhere.

Instinctively he checked out the security cameras. He knew where they all were, but Gary had schooled him to do it anyway in case something changed or he remembered wrong. These days, without even thinking, he was able to face away from their gaze or seek out their blind spots.

Something about the closest camera immediately caught his eye, though it took him a moment to decide what it was. Partly that was on account of how you should never let your gaze stop when you looked at cameras: the staff who watched the monitors picked up on that. The first time Gary had caught Clipper looking right into a camera he'd given him a right bollocking and then asked him if he'd got a watch. "Don't need it. I use my phone," Clipper had said.

The next day, Gary had handed him a watch. Nothing too flash because (remember, remember) you didn't want to stand out, but nice all the same. Gary explained that a watch was like a manacle and you wore one to show that you were one of the workers, a slave to the system, and therefore beneath notice. Then he asked Clipper whether he knew what a 'manacle' was. Clipper had felt like a right plum for saying he thought it was like a big sea-lion or something.

Gary explained, "If you find you've been staring at a camera, look at your watch like this," he made a little surprised face, "and get moving. Or if you want to change direction, 'cos maybe you've spotted someone you want to avoid, look at your watch first. The drones look at their watches constantly because their time belongs to someone else. Do the same and it's like camouflage: they won't see you."

'Drones' was another Gary-word; it referred to ordinary working punters. Clipper reckoned it probably came from the way they whined on endlessly about their jobs.

Clipper glanced at his watch now – it was almost a compulsive tic by this point – and then he let his gaze roam as though he was maybe putting together some talking points for the next budget meeting or something. This time as his eyes swept across the camera he realised what was weird. The cable that should run to the back of it ended about ten inches from the case. Had it been like that this morning when he came through? Had he just not noticed before?

He drifted down the platform, looking for the coppers, and interested to see if the other cameras were hooked up properly. If there was some refit going on and there was no surveillance at the moment it was a golden opportunity to get a little bit of a nicking spree going.

One minute now until the next train. From the times of the other trains it looked like the tube network was running slow today. No problem for him, of course, but it meant you had to plan your getaways a little more carefully.

Clipper reached the next camera just as he saw one of the coppers tucked behind a pillar up ahead of him, almost as though he was hiding.

The camera down this end was even more obviously out of action. Well, 'obvious' if you bothered to look, which no one ever did. There was a crack across the lens that Clipper could see from thirty feet away.

Gary claimed he'd once paid two kids fifty quid to bust all the cameras in Old Street tube using catapults and ball bearings. And then while the staff chased them round the station, Gary had lifted some designer's courier bag which contained a Mac laptop, one of the metal-skinned ones with all the extras on it, a PDA, a video iPod stacked with tunes and a touch-screen phone from Japan. Clipper suspected that the haul might have grown a little in the retelling, but still it was a sweet score. He looked around now for any signs that someone was working a similar scam. He didn't see any little Dennis the Menace types with catapults.

Clipper was also looking for the other copper and was momentarily troubled to see that he'd unknowingly walked past him, because he too was tucked away like the first one. Clipper was now sandwiched between them, which he didn't like, and what was worse was that the copper in front of him was looking right at him now.

Could they be here for him? Why had they split up and flanked him like that? And why was this first copper staring at him?

The familiar sound of an incoming train grew louder and Clipper tried not to meet the copper's gaze; he tried to look nonchalant, but it was difficult. He could hardly pretend he hadn't noticed a bloke in full SWAT regalia eyeballing him. Despite himself he found himself locking eyes with the man.

And a realisation stole over him like a hot flush. He looked totally different without hair. And in bulky tactical gear instead of a Paul Smith suit. And Clipper would have sworn he had a big, angry scar underneath one eye before which was gone now, but it was clearly the same bloke. The bloke he'd seen Gary getting his orders from. Warren. And he hadn't been a copper then, according to the few snippets Gary had let slip about him. Not unless coppers drove Aston Martins, spoke Chinese on the phone and paid other people to break the law for them. Which sort of suggested, to Clipper's rapidly whirring brain, if he hadn't been a copper before then he probably wasn't one now. Because there was being undercover, and then there was just out and out being a crook who owned a police uniform. Which did sort of beg the question of what was going on here and whether Clipper might be any part of it.

And at that moment the train came rumbling into the station and the men either side of Clipper started to close in on him.

***

Clipper remembered the first time he'd seen Gary in action. It was nine-thirty in the morning and the trains were still packed – all sorts of hold-ups earlier meant lots of people were still on their way to work. A scrum was pressing toward the open door of a stuffed train that had no more room for them inside. Gary was in the thick of it and Clipper saw him take a step back, because he didn't actually want to board the train, but he tipped his head back with a 'tut' as though it was someone else's fault, like he'd been elbowed aside.

"Can you all move along inside please," Gary called out, in a firm, pleasant voice that Clipper didn't recognise. Was there a Gary in some alternative universe somewhere who talked like that all the time? A teacher maybe.

The announcement came: "Stand clear of the doors please. Stand clear of the closing doors. This train is about to depart."

Gary did it again, allowed himself to be pushed back and let the annoyance register on his face. It was clear that no one else was going to get on board and most of the other punters were pulling back now, positioning themselves for the next train. Gary was still apparently optimistic though, attempting to insert a shoulder into the compressed mass of bodies. But it wasn't going to work.

The doors began to close and Gary retreated just enough to get out of their way. Then the train started to move and Clipper noticed the expression of one of the blank faces squashed up against the window changing to a look of alarm. And as the carriage moved past him, Clipper saw that something was caught in the rubber seal of the doors. It was about ten inches of thin white cable with a shiny plug at the end.

He looked towards Gary, who raised his eyebrows with a little expression of triumph and let Clipper see the iPod he was concealing in his palm. It was about the sweetest lift Clipper had ever seen.

Gary subtly pocketed the smooth plastic brick and, with an exasperated look at his watch, broke free of the scrum. He came to Clipper's side. "*Telegraph* reader," Gary said, "Might have let him off if I thought he only read the sport. Bastard was eyeing the International News."

Like a fair percentage of what Gary said, Clipper couldn't fully decipher the meaning, but he gave an appreciative chuckle. Gary always liked to explain why his marks deserved it.

"That was perfect," Clipper said, still amazed at how beautifully the whole thing had been executed.

"Not perfect," corrected Gary. "It's about time we talked about escape routes. When we're done, you'll see how this lift could be even better."

Then Gary had asked him to imagine what would happen if he stole a trog's wallet in plain view and then jumped on a train. "Just to make it more interesting," Gary said, "imagine you're wearing a t-shirt that says 'Thief' on it."

Clipper didn't really have to think about it. He said, "Well, they'd radio ahead to the next station, wouldn't they? Have someone collar me. Have them look out for the t-shirt."

"But what if you don't get off at the next station?" Gary asked. "Would they stop the train and search it?"

Clipper thought about the manpower involved and the disruption to the network and shook his head. "They'd probably only do that if it was a bomb or something."

Gary looked pleased with him. "So even if the trog asks everyone on the network to look out for you, you could still be anywhere. And even if they alert someone on every ticket barrier in London you could still get out using one of the fire exits or the old tunnels or through a substation. Mind you, there's a couple of stations where jumping on a train might not help." Plainly he wanted Clipper to work it out.

"Right before the end of the line," Clipper said, cheerily.

"Good," Gary said. "So look average and keep clear of platforms that lead you to the end of the line. Apart from that, if you've got the wind up, always choose a train over a platform."

They'd never got round to talking about how to improve the iPod lift Gary had demonstrated earlier and Clipper decided Gary wanted to 'leave it as an exercise for the reader', as he used to say – which meant Clipper was supposed to think it through on his own time.

***

Back in the present, the train had pulled in and Clipper was relieved to realise that Warren was no longer staring at him; he was scrutinising the train, scanning the passengers as they started to emerge. For a moment, Clipper took this as a sign: they were obviously not interested in him; they were after someone else, probably someone leaving the train. But then he glanced over his shoulder to see the other fake cop creeping up on him and he bolted. *Always choose a train over a platform,* Gary had taught him. Since Warren was hiding himself from the passengers behind one of the platform's massive pillars, Clipper headed for the other side of it and sprinted for the rear of the train.

Everyone else had finished getting on or off and Clipper had a clear path to the doors. He dashed for the rearmost double-set, and he'd almost made it when a thin man carrying a heavy briefcase came rushing out at the last minute and the two of them nearly collided.

Muttering an apology, Clipper skidded around him, scrambled inside the train, and looked nervously behind him for signs of pursuit. He couldn't see either of the fake coppers.

The thin man had slipped and was recovering himself. He leant on the edge of the door and peered out while adjusting his glasses, and tried to follow Clipper's gaze to see what he was running from.

"Is someone chasing you?" he asked, looking pretty unhappy about the possibility.

Clipper didn't respond immediately; he was much more interested in Warren and his sidekick than the man in front of him. The beeping sound that warned passengers that the doors were about to close was sounding as he absentmindedly answered, "Cops. Only they're not cops."

The slim man with the bag looked startled, and as the doors began to close, he pulled himself back inside the train, clutching the big, old-fashioned briefcase to his chest.

He was in his late twenties or early thirties, with wiry red-brown hair and he looked like a late-blooming grad student. His pale, checked shirt and scuffed corduroy jacket were from an earlier era – probably acquired from a previous generation of students by way of a charity shop. Fleetingly, Clipper wondered what his story was. Perhaps he was the fake-cops' real target and Clipper needn't have bolted. On the other hand, in Clipper's mind, Warren was high up on the list of people who might be behind Gary's disappearance (death? murder?) and therefore someone very much to be avoided. *Better safe than sorry*. If he'd bolted unnecessarily he could have a laugh about it once he was about twenty miles away sipping a cappuccino.

The doors closed with a bump, and Clipper and the weedy grad student both relaxed a little. Clipper realised their expressions were mirror images of each other and it almost made him laugh. But then a second later, Warren slammed heavily into the doors, stuck the fingertips of both hands into the rubber seal where the doors met, pulled them towards him and hauled them open again. Clipper hadn't thought you could do that.

Some part of the door mechanism agreed and was groaning and squealing in protest.

Clipper backed away, but the grad student was even more rattled. He ran to the back of the carriage, as far to the rear of the train as it was possible to get. The seats in that section were all empty, but the few passengers over on the far side of the doors were looking up in surprise, unsure what was going on.

Clipper wondered what the driver would do, whether he'd stop the train, but then he remembered that the driver relied on the platform cameras to be working to see what was going on. And for whatever reason, they were suddenly all out of action.

Warren's gaze was now fixed very firmly on the grad student. Warren may or may not have recognised Clipper earlier, but his reason for being there was obviously the thin man with the glasses and the battered briefcase.

Then the second fake-cop pounded up, stopping just behind Warren. Clipper considered the possibility that it was only Warren who was the fake, but he couldn't imagine a real copper teaming up with an impostor and not figuring it out. Surely they were both crooks.

"Tian, hold the doors," Warren said, slipping in through the gap he'd opened and leaving it to the man behind him to prevent them from closing again.

An announcement came over the train's speakers: "This is the driver speaking. I can't see who's playing silly buggers, but would whoever is preventing the doors from closing kindly stop it so we can all get on our way. Thank you." The 'thank you' was delivered in what Clipper thought of as textbook tube drivers' sarcasm.

Meanwhile Warren was advancing on the terrified grad student who was pressed against the back wall of the carriage. The only thing behind him was the rear driver's cab of the train, which would be empty at the moment, and beyond that open track. He looked very much like he wanted to push himself through the locked doors behind him and sprint away down the tunnel into the darkness.

"You're Kieran, aren't you?" Warren said, addressing the terrified man. "We're not here to hurt you, Kieran. We want what you're carrying and we want you to come with us." Then he glanced over his shoulder at the concerned passengers watching him and added, "Down to the station."

Kieran said nothing. So Warren took a step forwards. "Realistically, Kieran, you don't have anywhere else to go," he said pleasantly.

Kieran slipped a hand into the open top of his old-fashioned briefcase and began rummaging around, his search complicated by the fact that his eyes never left Warren's face.

Warren smiled, albeit without much warmth, and began to advance upon Kieran, who was thrashing his hand around inside the bag, desperate to locate something. A moment later he had it, and he withdrew his hand to reveal a fist clamped whitely around the grip of a gun. He snatched back the slide, chambering a bullet and raising the hammer. Several of the passengers on the far side of Clipper drew in their breath sharply enough that it sounded like a collective sigh. Someone whispered to herself, "Oh my god."

The driver was once again trying to close the doors and automated beeping filled the carriage as Warren adjusted to the presence of the gun. His smile finally gained some real warmth.

"What," he asked, "do you imagine you're going to do with that?"

Clipper, who was still in the little standing area by the doors, had lowered himself so that most of his body was screened by the row of seats nearest him. There was a piece of plate glass above him which gave standing passengers something to lean against and he peered cautiously through it now. He was aware that he was only a metre or so from the other fake-cop, but couldn't think of anything better to do than kind of cower where he was. It was what everyone else was doing.

Warren was apparently unconcerned, possibly even amused, at having a gun pointed at him. But at the same time he looked like he'd lost patience with the conversational approach; he took several brisk steps towards the armed man just as the annoyed train driver began making another announcement.

Kieran flinched at Warren's approach and simultaneously fired his gun, sending a bullet ricocheting off the roof above Warren's head; Clipper had no idea where it ended up. A moment later Kieran composed himself and fired point blank at Warren, who seemed to stagger slightly, but gave no sign that the bullet had penetrated his flak jacket. *You can't hurt them*, Clipper found himself thinking.

Surely the driver would hear the gunshot. Inside the carriage the sound of the shot had been tremendous. But the driver was several hundred feet away, in his own little cab, in the middle of making another announcement. Clipper realised that whatever sound made it through the gap in the partly-opened doors would probably be swallowed by the vast space of the station. From where the driver sat, the gunshot would have all the volume of a distant door slamming or a shutter coming down.

As Clipper watched, Warren had almost reached Kieran. Then Kieran fired a third time, his composure gone, this shot even wilder than the first. Glass exploded and Clipper gave an involuntary moan of fear, recoiling as splinters of shattered plate glass sprayed across his face and shoulder, pattering into his hair and rattling across the floor around him.

But it wasn't the partition on Clipper's side of the carriage that had been hit; it was the one by the partly open doors. And now Clipper was turning his head and looking up at the second fake copper who'd been twisted around by the impact of the bullet, which looked to have caught him somewhere around where his neck met his shoulder. As well as being shot, he'd also been raked by pellets of glass as the bullet punched through the plate glass screen beside him. Beneath one of his eyes blood welled like red tears. He made a slow deep sound of surprise and pain, like a groan.

Warren looked round and yelled, "Sebastian!" as the driver's announcement concluded – no one had heard a word of it – and then Sebastian toppled sideways and slammed to the floor beside Clipper, allowing the doors to clatter shut behind him.

Warren threw a murderous glance at Kieran, who visibly recoiled, and then he rushed to Sebastian's side while Clipper tried to shrink further into the corner, willing himself to be invisible.

Warren crouched by Sebastian's side. He was oblivious to Kieran, who'd taken a halting step forwards and kind of let himself half slump into the seat nearest him. Kieran looked like he was deciding whether to have a heart attack or not. His face was difficult to read, a blend of fear and uncertainty, and maybe some surprise at what he'd just done. He was still holding the gun in his outstretched arm and he looked twitchy enough to do just about anything. He was also… Clipper wasn't sure, but he watched, his gaze operating on autopilot, as Kieran's free hand moved across the upholstery of the seat beside him while his eyes stayed fixed on Warren. There was something in Kieran's hand, a tiny blade of some kind, that was slicing into the heavy fabric. Clipper's eyes seemed to track Kieran's clandestine movements of their own accord while his thoughts remained jumbled and panicky, thrown into a tangle by the shooting.

A metre or so from Clipper, Sebastian was trying to speak. Warren held his head up slightly which seemed to help. After a moment's effort Sebastian said, "I was just moving my shield to hold the doors." He tried to give a shrug. "Bad timing. I'm sorry."

The bullet had struck only a few seconds before but there was already a lot of blood on the floor. Sebastian had his hand pressed against the base of his neck, but vivid blood welled in pulses between his fingers. His eyes were flickering with pain and concentration.

Then, with a lurch, the train finally began to move and Warren glanced up as he registered the change. A groan from Sebastian brought his attention straight back to his wounded friend. "You have to stop the bleeding," he said, squeezing the man's arm to emphasise his words. "Concentrate."

Clipper, still pressed into his corner, was holding perfectly still. He was trying orient his thoughts, to figure out what was happening, what he should be doing – and for the moment he was having no success at all. He was aware that the train was moving, aware that an armed man had opened fire in this carriage, aware that someone had been hit, but he wasn't sure how to process any of it.

And for a moment he was back in that club, waiting for Gary, seeing Warren turn, and watching a broken bottle grind itself to pieces on the empty space in front of him, watching a punch that never landed slam his attacker to the floor.

Gary had said you couldn't hurt them, whoever *they* were. But surely this was one of them, lying at Clipper's feet, his blood leaking out onto the floor of the train, the spreading pool even now reaching the toe of Clipper's scuffed right shoe. The man was going to bleed to death while Clipper crouched, really only inches away, immobile, within the growing circle of his blood, and something about that seemed so wrong that it set him in motion.

Before he knew what he was doing, Clipper found himself speaking. "Pressure. We need to put pressure on the wound," he said.

Warren looked round at him and just stared.

Clipper was pulling off his tie, winding it round his hand and threading the end through to make a ball of material. He came slightly out of his crouch, eyes flicking nervously towards the man with the gun and then back to the piercing look on Warren's face, wondering all the while who he should be most afraid of.

"I could…" He held up the wad of material to show his intention. Warren's stare didn't slacken.

After a pause, the stare lengthening, Warren said coldly, "I know you, don't I?"

Just what I need, Clipper thought to himself, *more stress*. But he knew what to say. Another of Gary's tutorials had covered this. At Gary's suggestion, they had dreamed up half a dozen responses to this question, intended to be given to trogs, coppers and previous victims, should anyone recognise them. Clipper picked the first one that came to mind.

"My brother maybe. He does adverts. Posters and stuff. Like those crunchy cornflakes," he said and shrugged. It occurred to him that if he pretended not to be afraid of Warren it would make this easier, and might defuse Warren's suspicion. Because Clipper had a sneaking feeling that anyone who truly knew Warren would be permanently afraid.

Clipper was trying to reach Sebastian now, but Warren hadn't shifted aside, though his hostility had disappeared somewhat and for a moment he seemed lost in thought.

Then a voice by Clipper's ear said, "Let me help." And it was the girl from the plaza, the one with hair the colour of maple syrup, the one he'd spoken to. And he remembered their conversation, how much he'd enjoyed it, and how it seemed like it had happened at least a week ago.

***

Rachel hung up. That was the fun part over. She'd burned her bridges with some real gusto and now she wouldn't be able to back out or change her mind. But wasn't that why people used to burn bridges? Or was it ships? Whatever. They were burned.

Putting her relationship with Rudy to the torch had been particularly easy, once she knew she had nothing to lose. As a boss he'd been a disaster and now there was no reason to pretend otherwise; she'd laid it out for him. Ticked off his faults with chilly efficiency. It was a talent she'd inherited from her mother – what she thought of as the family curse. Whatever you called it, she had her mother's blistering forthrightness, even in German. Which was why she'd been putting off this second call for weeks. Putting it off until after she'd resigned. Putting it off until after she'd booked her plane tickets home. Putting it off until her last day at work, until her transatlantic flight was only hours away.

Time to call home.

No one had ever accused her or her mother of being two-faced, or of keeping quiet about other people's shortcomings. Her mother never got calls from old friends saying, "Why weren't you straight with me?" Naturally the main reason for that was her mother's total lack of old friends. But if any had stuck around long enough to give their opinion, they'd have told you: she was so straight with people it made your eyes water.

There was no puzzle to it; Rachel could see it quite clearly: her mother's way with people, the effect it had on them, and the woman's inability to follow the logic of her own bluntness all the way through to the damage it caused. And even though it seemed so obvious when she looked at her mother's life, she suspected that she had exactly the same faults and exactly the same blind-spot, the same obliviousness to consequences.

It never felt wrong, letting rip like that, hitting them right between the eyes. It felt pure and honest and simple. But it wasn't anywhere near as exhilarating sitting around waiting for them to come back, waiting for them to get over the initial sting of hearing the truth, and gradually realising that they never would.

Before she'd come to London, around the time that she realised living with her mother was no longer remotely bearable, Rachel had done her best to get through to her, to make her understand that she was driving everyone around her away. And she hadn't been a hundred percent surprised when her mother failed to acknowledge the truth of it – but had instead repaid the compliment by rounding on her, proceeding to enumerate all the ways in which Rachel herself was deficient, deluded or unlikable. It was quite a fight.

There hadn't been much left to say after that. Or rather neither of them were interested in saying it. So that's how they'd left it. Their relationship a lifeless, radioactive wasteland. Emotional Chernobyl.

It wasn't until Rachel had been in London a few weeks and had looked back calmly on that last unrestrained, fully-nuclear exchange that she'd understood what had happened, the forces that had been at work. Her own certainty that she was right and her mother's monstrously stubborn refusal to admit it were two sides of the same coin. Her mother would have been feeling the same chill, thin wind of righteousness roaring through her and marvelling at the pigheaded obstinacy of the woman in front of her. Really, the whole thing was just her mother having a fight with her own reflection; Rachel was simply the vessel by which this stupidity could annihilate itself and simultaneously pass down to the next generation.

She had no idea what the solution was – it couldn't be dishonesty or blandness – she couldn't very well start simpering, it would be more than she could bear – but equally there had to be a way of wielding the truth that didn't involve using it to mug anyone who wouldn't take the hint and drift away of their own accord. The furthest she'd got in her search for an answer was the beginnings of a suspicion that it had something to do with trust. Maybe her caustic honesty was just about getting her retaliation in first. Maybe if you could really be sure of someone, you didn't need to launch pre-emptive strikes. Now if only she could persuade her mother of that.

Slowly she dialled her mother's number. In her heart it was still *her* number too. Pushing the keys one by one felt like arming a bomb. A thought occurred to her: what if her mother no longer got up this early? Conversational bloodshed would be inevitable. *Oh well*. Rachel tried to pull together a few words that might produce some effect besides silence or a long-distance brawl. At the other end, the phone rang: long American tones.

"Hello?" It was her mother's voice. The first time she'd heard it in almost three years.

She let her breath out and spoke: "Hi Mom."

There was silence at the other end of the line and Rachel cupped her other hand around the phone to keep the wind away from the mouthpiece.

"Hi," her mom said eventually. Her tone gave nothing away.

"Mom, I…" How could she possibly phrase this? There was no easy way to express it. But then an unexpected swell of emotion pushed words out of her mouth: "Mom, the thing is… I miss you and I'd like to come home."

She hadn't said 'want' to come home, but 'like'. It wasn't a demand. She was throwing herself on her mother's mercy. A quality her mother had never given any sign of possessing.

More than anything Rachel had ever done, this felt like putting her neck on the block and waiting for the axe to fall. The first thing her mother would do was ask what this meant, what it signified. She'd want it spelled out that Rachel was capitulating, admitting that she'd been wrong. Then she'd lay down some rules about how it was going to be different this time – and by different she'd mean tighter, tougher, more under control, with less room for future rebellions.

Rachel could almost hear her speak the words: "So what are you saying? You've come to your senses at last? Well, let me tell you…" But those words never came.

Instead: "Are you…" Her mother's voice was strange. "Are you OK? Is everything OK?" Her mother seemed unsure. Rachel wasn't sure she'd ever heard her sound like that before.

This was unexpected, but it was too soon to relax; fighting could still break out at any moment. But the fact it hadn't yet was more than Rachel had expected.

"I'm fine," Rachel said carefully. "I'm quitting this job, though. I *have* quit it." She regretted saying it like that. 'Quitting' was a trigger phrase of her mother's. Not something she had ever permitted.

Her mother said nothing.

Rachel went on: "It's just that… I miss you and I miss the horses too." It was silly but true. "I don't know how things are, if they've changed, but if you… if it's OK with you, I want to come home. Help with the farm. See how it goes."

Her mother still said nothing. The pause lengthened.

Rachel spoke into the silence. "So might you, um… I mean, *is* it OK if I come home?" Her mother was really making her work for this, but Rachel wasn't going to chicken out now, no matter how agonising it was to say these things aloud. She'd been prepared for battle. She'd been determined not to provoke it, but she'd been expecting it. So she wasn't going to let the silent treatment throw her off track.

Then she realised her mother was crying. "Mom?" she asked, wondering if something had happened. Had someone died? Was something else wrong, besides their screwed-up relationship?

"Come home, honey," her mother said, between sobs. "I was scared you would never call. I couldn't bear it. Just come home and we'll make it work out."

"Really?" Rachel said, hope rising inside her. She felt stupid for making her mom repeat herself, and about five years old. But this was beyond her wildest expectations. "Are you OK? Is everything OK? I'm going to be home tomorrow sometime, if it's alright."

She could hear happiness in her mother's voice now, even though she was sniffling and her words were thick with emotion: "Everything's fine. Just come home. The horses miss you. Me too."

"I'll see you tomorrow," Rachel said. "We can… never mind. I'll see you tomorrow."

She hung up, feeling amazed and bewildered. And then a wave of relief washed over her so profound that she felt tears start to gather in her eyes, pooling along her lower lids and making the ground beneath her look blurred and indistinct. She blinked, and hot droplets ran down the cold skin of her cheeks. And then someone was talking to her, asking her if she was OK and she turned to tell him that she felt fantastic.

She smiled up at him. "I'm giving up a job I hate and I'm going back home. And my mom actually said she wanted to see me. So I'm fine thanks," she gushed, taking in the young man in front of her: scruffy, mid-twenties, OK looking, and with the most amazing look of concern on his face.

"You hate your job?" he said, as though he'd never come across the idea before. "What do you do?" he asked, sounding troubled.

"Well, there's the long version, but pretty much if you boil it down, I would say that I was a thief," she said. "Yes. That's it: a thief. Why, what do you do?" She didn't know quite why she was having this conversation, but he'd seemed so worried for her and he'd chosen a moment when her defences were absolutely down.

"I'm… well, I'm a thief too," he said. "Only I really am."

She smiled and sniffed away the last tear. "OK. Well, I'm pleased to meet you. I'm Rachel," she said.

"Matt," he said and stuck out his hand and they shook. With the formalities, it sort of felt like they were playing at being grown-ups. But somehow it was a good game.

"I love the name Rachel," he said.

"From *Friends*?" she asked him, narrowing her moist eyes.

"Nah," he said, "*Blade Runner*."

"You know that Rachel means 'ewe'?" she said.

"Ewww?" he asked, unsure.

"Exactly," she said, laughing. The conversation with her mother had released so much tension she felt almost high. She could talk to anyone about anything right now.

"You're really a thief?" she asked.

"Yup," Matt said. "Sorry."

"You like it?" she asked.

That seemed to stop him in his tracks. "I used to," he told her, and then he frowned. "It used to be exciting and I honestly didn't feel like I was really hurting anyone. But something's changed. I think I might have had enough."

"That," said Rachel triumphantly, "is precisely how I feel."

He lowered his head a little and said quietly, "But I don't know what else to do."

He looked like a little boy when he said it. Rachel wanted to wrap her arms around him. Her emotions were all mixed up, the wonderful warmth of relief still spreading through her, making this strange conversation seem lighter than air.

"Come home with me," she said enthusiastically. The words just popped out, like something in a dream. Surely she'd only thought them, not said them out loud? None of this felt quite real. She found herself asking, "You any good with horses?"

He looked surprised. "I don't know," he said. "I mean yes. I had a weekend job at a stables when I was living in California with my dad. And right now, when I think about it, that seems like the best thing I ever did. You've… have you got horses, then?"

She nodded. "My mom's farm in Oregon. It's beautiful there." She smiled at the thought and then looked down at the two huge bags by her feet. "It's where I'm going right now."

But when she looked up, he wasn't staring at her anymore. All through this dream-like conversation he hadn't looked away from her for an instant – she wasn't even sure he'd blinked. But now his gaze had flicked past her, over her shoulder.

"Listen, I…" he started. "I'm glad you're alright."

She wanted to say something, to stop him leaving – she had no idea what, but she didn't want this extraordinary conversation to come to an end. She opened her mouth, but no words came to mind.

"I've gotta go," he said and then he was gone, threading through the crowd, glancing back a couple of times, though not towards her.

Abruptly, she realised how cold it was outside. And she felt weird, but not good weird – sort of sick actually. Somehow the talk she'd had with Matt, wonderful though it had been, had left her with a sour feeling of loss that threatened to spoil the incredible elation she'd felt after things had gone so well with her mother. She tried to remember exactly how she'd felt when she'd hung up, the sense of enveloping calm, the way her anxiety had dissolved away leaving behind tears and a warmth that might have been love. It was still there, but somehow the moment was gone. Her encounter with Matt had spoiled it, which was ridiculous because she'd loved every second of their strange little talk. It was the sudden way it had ended. She felt cheated.

She was angry – and angry at her anger. She picked up her bags and moved towards the station entrance. This silly irritation would fade, wouldn't it? She would forget about the ridiculous conversation with the man who'd told her he was a thief. Then she'd have the whole long slow flight to Seattle to picture her mother's face and how it would look when Rachel walked into her kitchen. At last, after nearly three years, she could actually imagine her mother's face smiling back at her.

***

Now Rachel was crouching next to Clipper and talking to Warren. She was trying to avoid presenting a target to the gunman and she'd taken off her jacket. "I'm afraid that's arterial blood. It'll need surgery. But we can help a little if we sit him up and do like… um… Matt said." Clipper cringed slightly to hear Rachel telling Warren his real name.

She caught his eye and he wasn't sure if there was some message she was trying to send or whether she just wanted to acknowledge his presence.

She went on: "Yeah, like Matt said: pressure, and sit him up. Can you radio to the next station and get an ambulance on its way?" Her voice was calm, though Clipper could see a little sheen of moisture on her upper lip. She'd folded her jacket and was slipping it behind Sebastian's head. She'd had to lean across Clipper to do it and absentmindedly he realised that she did in fact smell fantastic, just as he'd imagined.

Warren didn't reply. He'd moved aside slightly to give her room, but he seemed totally distracted, circulating in his own thoughts. And then a moment later he was back. The hard look dropping into place like a visor. The momentary indecisiveness was gone.

He leaned over his fallen companion. "Sebastian," he said evenly, "I think this might not work out."

Clipper could see that something was missing that had been there earlier. The concern was gone. He looked down at his partner with eyes that were hooded and blank. He seemed to have reached some sort of verdict on the situation. The set of his features suggested that it wasn't a particularly charitable one.

Now his gaze left Sebastian and flicked for a moment towards Kieran. Then he turned to Rachel and Clipper. "Look after him," he said, flatly, like he was speaking to a servant. "I have work to do." That last remark was addressed to himself as much as to them.

Then he stood, leaving the wounded man to their care – but he ignored Kieran; instead he turned the other way, facing the few remaining passengers in the compartment.

Kieran still reacted to his movement with a start, rapidly pushing off the seat he'd been leaning against and jerking himself to his feet, gun extended. But he needn't have bothered; at that moment no one was paying him any attention.

Now Warren stood squarely, balancing easily against the motion of the carriage, and called out over the racket of the train to the three other people in the compartment. They were all crouching at the front end of the carriage, as far from both the injured cop and the gunman as possible. They'd pressed themselves into the corner, right by the door that led to the next compartment.

"I want you three to move towards the front of the train. Tell everyone you meet that there is a serious police situation back here and get them to move away. Everything is under control, more men are on the way, but when I look through those windows…" he pointed towards the next compartment, "I don't want to see any members of the public. Do you understand? Just leave everything to us, don't complicate the situation, and get everyone else to safety."

"Not you," he added firmly but quietly, addressing Clipper and Rachel.

The retreating passengers scrambled to get the connecting door open without exposing themselves to a direct shot. They didn't seem to notice that Kieran was oblivious to anyone but Warren. As they slammed the door behind them, Clipper thought he detected a change in the motion of the train. It was slowing. But from experience he knew they weren't at the next station yet. Either the driver knew that something was wrong… or maybe more likely, it was one of the thousand little delays the underground system experienced every day. Then the train's speed levelled out. They'd slowed down somewhat but it didn't seem like they were stopping. *Probably just congestion*, thought Clipper, *and not help on its way*. Then he turned his attention back to Warren.

Warren waited until the retreating passengers were a good distance into the next carriage before he finally turned back to face Kieran. Their eyes locked, and Kieran stepped back, involuntarily, before quickly correcting the aim of his gun. Then Warren began moving purposefully towards him with a heavy, steady walk that put Clipper in mind of a tank rolling into position. Warren looked like it would take more than a few bullets to stop him.

"If you put that gun down now I won't kill you," he said reasonably, as he advanced on the other man. His voice was low, just enough to carry over the noise of the train, but Clipper and Rachel could hear him.

Back behind the seats, Clipper saw Rachel's uncertain frown. It was easy for him to forget that she'd still got some catching up to do. Warren's words were obviously bothering her. They weren't exactly standard cop-speak. Warren's tone had been… well, the best word was probably 'sinister'. If you added in the fact he seemed to think he was bullet-proof, Clipper could see there was plenty to frown about.

He didn't exactly have all the answers, but Clipper felt he should share the little he did know. He looked down at Sebastian, whose eyes were flickering, half closed, his pupils twitching and unfocused. He gave no sign that he was paying attention to them, so Clipper leant across and whispered to Rachel, "Yeah, they're not really cops." He hadn't meant it to sound cocky.

He looked at her face to see if she'd understood him. Her eyes were wide and questioning – demanding that he say more. He put his mouth close to her ear and whispered, "I don't know much about them, but they're crooks. The uniforms… it's all fake." He was still keeping his voice low, though Sebastian had yet to give any sign he was aware of them.

A few metres away, Warren had halted. He was explaining the situation to Kieran: "Think about how much harm I could have done to you by now if I'd wanted to, but you haven't got a scratch on you. That's because I want you to talk to us, tell us who you've been working with. And for that, I want you in one piece. Isn't that what you want too?" His hands were spread in a gesture that was probably intended to be non-threatening and patient. But Warren's expression altogether spoiled the effect. If he'd had his face chromed it couldn't have displayed less warmth.

"You're really making this difficult," he said and it seemed like a little sarcasm might be creeping into his tone. He paused for a moment to let Kieran respond to his offer. Then he added, "Imagine all the ways this could end. There's only one version in which you're still breathing. And it's the one where you cooperate with me."

His words seemed to be getting to Kieran, who was really sweating now, and shifting awkwardly. He took a faltering step towards Warren, his gun lowering slightly, unsure, as though his determination was wavering. It almost looked like he was giving up.

On the other hand, Clipper could see the tension in Kieran's body. Even the arm that had dropped slightly was so taut it trembled. If his tendons had been any tighter Clipper reckoned you'd be able to play a tune on them. As it was, he could almost hear Kieran's body humming with tension. He couldn't decide whether the man was about to give up or hurl himself physically at Warren.

Whether Warren was fooled or not by the show of uncertainty, Clipper couldn't say, but a moment later the pretence was over. Having shuffled forwards a little, Kieran twisted around and fired two rapid shots into the door lock behind him. Then he snapped back towards Warren, keeping the gun trained on him, while using his other hand to snatch his bag from the seat beside him. Gun outstretched, he shoved himself backwards, bursting through the door behind and nearly toppling into the gloom of the deserted rear cab of the train.

Clipper was fairly sure you didn't need to shoot those cab doors open; there was a release-lever that passengers could use in an emergency; but he had to admit, the gun was quicker. Plus, if you already had a weapon in your hand in a situation like this, your survival instincts probably dictated that you didn't put it down while you fiddled with a door lock.

Kieran took two quick and stumbling steps backwards into the rear cab, but instead of going after him, Warren hesitated for a moment and Clipper found himself wondering about that. He was getting the distinct impression that whatever protected Warren and Sebastian from harm, it was at its least effective when they were moving. But then as soon as Kieran had disappeared into the dark of the cab, Warren dashed forwards to close with him.

Kieran must have expected this because simultaneously his arm came halfway up, lifting up out of the darkness of the rear cab, while the rest of him remained in shadow. The gun fired again, this time angled straight down at Warren's feet. The outstretched arm vanished into the darkness as Warren cried out and snatched his right foot away, slipping and falling back across the seats behind him. It was an ugly fall, with Warren's lower back coming down hard on the solid jutting edge of an armrest. His attempts to break his fall tipped him sideways almost head-first onto the vinyl-coated floor of the train. He lay there for a moment hardly moving.

Clipper craned his head and saw a splatter of blood on the floor and a chunk punched out of Warren's right boot. Clipper didn't know how serious getting shot in the foot was in the relative scheme of things, but even as he watched, Warren was scrambling to right himself, so it couldn't have been too bad. For his part, though, Clipper found the violence of it shocking. He was getting the definite impression that you needed to see a lot more than two people get shot in front of your eyes before it became something you could manage to be casual about.

'Shock' captured the feeling perfectly; for a moment you just couldn't believe it had happened. But while most of Clipper's brain was recoiling from the noise of gunfire and the terror of being trapped in a confined space watching people on either side of him get shot, another more analytical part of his mind was trying to learn something useful from what he'd seen.

For a second Clipper wondered if he was going to be able to think his way out of this situation: figure out what Warren's limitations were, what his agenda was, and use that knowledge to time a rapid exit. If he was really lucky Warren and Kieran would still be trying to kill each other when the train reached the next station and then he could just grab Rachel by the arm and run like hell.

He glanced at over at her, wondering if she was doing the same thing, trying to think this all through. It was hard to tell. She looked frightened – but then maybe he did too – but she wasn't looking panicked. He thought about how she'd moved to his side after Sebastian was hit. She'd been shaken, but she'd had it under control. He wouldn't be surprised if her mind was working just as hard as his. Which gave him a fair bit of comfort because she was very likely a lot smarter than he was. If he was really honest with himself, thinking his way out of a situation was not something he'd ever shown much talent for, and these weren't exactly the ideal circumstances for him to perfect the skill. His friend Gary had always been the brains of the operation. He'd done his best to turn Clipper into a thinker, but it had been an uphill struggle for both of them. Even so, if Gary were here, he'd be urging Clipper to think: to work out ahead of time what the important moments were so that when they happened he'd be ready.

That, and research; Gary had always been very big on research. Which was why Clipper found his gaze flicking down to the pool of blood by his feet. He was staring at its colour. It was that familiar shade of red. Though it was maybe a little brighter and more orangey as it welled from Sebastian's neck, but Rachel had said that blood was 'arterial' – Clipper had no idea what that meant, unless it was something to do with arteries – but she seemed to recognise the look of it. Besides, you couldn't really judge under these lights. The point was that so far as he could tell,

Sebastian, and the blood he was losing such a lot of, were both human. He felt stupid for even questioning it, but what else was he to think?

But the twitching, delirious figure in front of him was bleeding what looked like real blood from what seemed like an honest-to-god bullet hole in his neck. He was pretty obviously human and he was pretty obviously dying, unless he got some proper medical attention. And now Warren had been hurt too. So whatever else Sebastian and Warren were, they were also men. It was one simple and solid fact in an otherwise insane situation and it made Clipper feel just a tiny bit better.

That feeling of reassurance grew a little stronger as he watched the superman who was probably responsible for his best and only friend Gary's death slipping in a patch of his own blood as he tried to scramble back to his feet.

A moment later, Warren had hauled himself upright, clutching a handrail with one muscular arm while he held his perforated foot above the floor and swore. Under other circumstances it might have been gruesomely funny, but not here and now. Meanwhile Kieran had completely disappeared into the gloom of the empty rear cab. Peering towards the open door, Clipper could see part of a dark window, and beyond, the occasional tunnel light receding slowly down the track. Kieran was moving about in there, but Clipper couldn't see what he was doing. Panicking, most likely.

Warren took a few deep breaths, steadied himself against the lurching of the train, and put his weight on his damaged foot. The bleeding seemed to have stopped straightaway, though when he took his first step he quickly took a second one to get his good foot back under him. From the location of the hole, the bullet must have gone right through the middle of his boot and out through the sole. No wonder it was a little tender.

Warren had reached the open door of the rear cab and grabbed hold of the frame for support. Then he paused for a moment and called out ahead of him, "You're really not making this easy, Kieran. You're not even trying to keep on my good side, are you?" Then he winced and bent to fiddle with his boot, yanking at the laces.

By Clipper's side, Rachel moved closer and whispered in his ear, "So do you have any idea what the hell is going on?"

"I don't really know," Clipper whispered back. "But I mean *obviously* that bloke, Kieran, has crossed these people somehow. And you've seen they… they seem to have some sort of… power." He wasn't sure he was contributing anything so he stopped talking for a moment while he collected his thoughts. Then he tried again. "I've seen *that* one," he dropped his voice even further and indicated Warren, "before. I reckon he killed a friend of mine. And he wasn't a copper then; he was bent as a nine-bob note."

"I've got no idea what that means," Rachel said coldly. Then a minute later she asked suspiciously, "So who *are* you?"

"No one," Clipper said, being defensive. His whisper was more of a hiss: "I just nick things. So did my mate, Gary. Then he did some work for that guy, who called himself Warren. And right after that, my mate disappeared. I don't know any more than that. Except I saw Warren do that trick once before, where it's like he's indestructible. Though it obviously doesn't work the whole time. I also saw him knock someone down without touching them."

Rachel was taking this in without commenting. He reckoned the fact she'd seen Warren shot point-blank and not get hurt must be lending a bit of credibility to his ridiculous-sounding story.

He went on, "Warren knows he knows me, but he can't remember where from. I really only saw him once, just before Gary went missing." He saw Rachel's look become calculating and said, "Honestly, I don't think I'm anything to do with this. It's just a coincidence I'm here. I swear."

Rachel considered his words, but said nothing. They were silent for a moment, watching Warren wrestle with his boot before going in to tackle Kieran. Clipper spoke to Rachel again, "Look, I reckon now's your chance. Get to the door back there while he's busy."

She hesitated a moment and then shook her head. "He'd see me. And… leaving you on your own doesn't seem the right thing to do."

He said, "Yeah, well, that's very nice, but I'm sure you'd get over it. Go on, at least try."

She shook her head again. "Look, I don't see that either of them," she flicked her eye towards the cab, "are actually trying to hurt me. You go if you want," she said and nodded towards Sebastian, "but someone should look after him." Then she took the wadded tie from him and pressed it more firmly against Sebastian's wound, adding, "It's not like you're very good at first aid."

He couldn't tell if she was joking. He thought maybe she was trying; it was just difficult with all the adrenaline. He whispered, "And you are? I thought you swindled people for a living."

She shrugged and said, "Well… before the swindling I had a year of vet's school. OK?"

He didn't bother to reply to that. He could see how anyone listening to them might think they were arguing. It certainly sounded like it. But it didn't *feel* like it. It felt like they were agreeing to stay together for a little longer. Clipper was surprised at how much better that made him feel.

At the back of the carriage Warren was triumphantly pulling off his damaged boot. He tipped it up, allowing a thin trickle of blood to run out. Tossing the boot behind him, he stepped into the doorway of the rear cab. With one boot on and one off, he was walking like a peg-legged pirate, but the look on his face was serious enough.

With Warren blocking the doorway Clipper couldn't see exactly what happened next, but a moment later there was another gunshot, the flash lighting up the dim cab, but not for long enough to let Clipper see anything, and then there was a rushing noise which didn't go away – in fact a moment later it jumped in volume again. The train was suddenly much noisier and cold air was moving quickly through the compartment.

Clipper tried to peer past Warren to see what was happening. It looked like the door at the back of the rear cab was now open. Clipper was seeing straight out into the tunnel beyond and he could catch the occasional glimpse of Kieran flailing around. With a shock, Clipper realised he must be hanging off the rear of the train. Clipper caught a glimpse of him holding on with one hand, while the other struggled to clasp his briefcase to his chest.

Even though the train was travelling more slowly than normal, the steel rails were still sliding past at maybe thirty miles an hour and there was nothing either side of them but concrete. Without meaning to, Clipper found himself picturing what a collision with metal and masonry at that sort of speed would be like – never mind the six hundred volts of electricity crackling through the live rail.

He could hardly bear to watch. There didn't seem to be any way back for Kieran; he had pretty much run out of options. His one hope would be to stop resisting and plead with Warren to help him back onto the train. Otherwise it would only be a matter of time. But it didn't look like

Kieran was going to do that. Clipper's insides bunched at the thought of what came next.

And then, a moment later, his fears became real. Kieran pitched backwards and was snatched from sight, and Clipper could hardly stop himself from yelling out. He found he'd jammed the knuckles of his right hand into his mouth without realising it. From the glimpse he'd seen it was difficult to tell if Kieran had just lost his grip. It almost looked like he'd jumped. Clipper stared in disbelief for one very long second.

Then the moment passed and there was a bright spitting flash just beyond the rear of the train and fat, angry sparks filled the tunnel behind them. Clipper thought he heard a scream over the noise of the train, but he couldn't be sure. Then there was a loud wooden slap as all the brakes came on simultaneously and at the same moment all the lights in the train went out.

In total darkness, the train pitched beneath them as screeching wheels tried to bring several hundred of tons of metal to an instant halt. Broken glass and unidentified debris tumbled forwards. Blindly, Rachel gripped Clipper's arm in the dark and he reflexively grabbed onto her as they tried to avoid being flung across the carriage towards metal handrails and hard corners they could no longer see. She must have had hold of something solid because she was able to stop them both from being thrown around. Her unbreakable grip kept him from taking a dive headfirst into the dark.

Endless moments later the train had squealed and lurched to a final halt. And then, with the power off, it was abruptly silent – the sudden peace occasionally interrupted by pings, creaks and hisses as parts of the train cooled and contracted.

A few moments later emergency lights came on in the compartment and they could see again, though more dimly than before. It took Clipper a second or two to realise that his fingers were still digging deep into the flesh of Rachel's arm. It must have hurt like hell but she didn't show it. He released his grip and said, "God I'm sorry. I didn't realise. I was just trying to hold on."

"I know," she said, simple acceptance in her voice. Then she looked around, peering towards the rear cab. "Did you see what happened in there?" she asked. "Did he fall? I couldn't tell."

"I think he might even have jumped," Clipper said, "but I couldn't see properly." He realised how loud their voices sounded now.

Then he shrugged, without quite knowing why, and said a little more quietly, "I heard that you have a fifty-fifty chance of missing the live rail. We were going slowly; maybe he thought it was worth risking it." What he didn't add was that it really said something about Warren's reputation if the people he chased were willing to throw themselves off a moving train to get away from him.

As he finished speaking, it belatedly occurred to Clipper to wonder what had happened to Warren. Was he busy with something in the cab? Or maybe he'd fallen too? It hadn't looked like it, but perhaps Kieran had grabbed hold of him at the last moment and they'd tumbled onto the tracks together. Clipper couldn't help hoping that's what had taken place. But if Warren didn't appear soon, Clipper really was going to begin edging the pair of them towards the door to the next compartment.

And where was the driver? Shouldn't there be an announcement? Wouldn't the intercom system work even on emergency power?

Or maybe there was a limit to the number of bullets you could fire into a tube carriage before you broke something important. Gary was always telling him things about the trains and the Underground, and encouraging him to find out more. Now Clipper wished he'd followed up on that.

Despite all those unanswered questions, he found his thoughts kept coming back to Rachel. He studied her face. "So, are you OK?" he asked her. She was busy checking Sebastian over. She looked up at him without saying anything and he found he couldn't read her at that moment. Nevertheless, something about the feel of her eyes on his affected him, just like it had done when he'd first seen her. He found himself volunteering: "I'm sorry I ran off before, when we were outside."

She was staring at him now and her hands had stopped moving, though her face still gave no sign of what she was thinking. He explained, "I got a bit scared," and then he laughed, adding, "Seems silly compared to all this."

And finally he said, "It was… really good talking to you. I meant to say that to you. Before."

Rachel said nothing for a while and then spoke quietly: "I… know what you mean. You caught me off guard. It seemed like… there might have been… more for us to talk about." She was obviously even more awkward about putting this it into words than him.

Clipper's instinct was to make a joke: "But, you know, here we are. We got a chance to have another chat after all." He did his best to give her a smile, so she'd know he was trying to cheer her up. She snorted in a way that he read as meaning a smile in return was expecting too much but she appreciated the effort. After a moment, she returned her attention to Sebastian.

The train had been stationary for a full minute by now and Clipper had begun to wish he'd being doing something useful instead of talking. If he'd got them out of that carriage straightaway they could have been half way down the train by now. Whether that would have done them any good, was another question.

Rachel had finished making Sebastian comfortable. He was barely conscious. He'd been shaken around as the train's brakes had locked but Rachel had propped him up again, hoping to slow the bleeding a little, and was once more pressing the wadded tie to his neck. The pool of blood around him was ominously wide now. And splotches of it were starting to get everywhere – on their shoes and clothes. Rachel's hands and dark blouse were streaked with it and a dark red smudge had somehow made its way to her forehead. Clipper tried to guess at the volume of blood. He found he had to imagine it was some more familiar liquid before he could even begin to work out how much you'd have to spill to make that much mess. It had to be more than a pint. Probably more like two.

"What do you think we should do?" Clipper asked. "I know he's in a pretty bad state," he nodded towards Sebastian, "but I *really* don't trust these people. I still think we should make a run for it."

Rachel was obviously working it through in her mind. After a minute she said, "Listen Matt, you don't know what that guy Kieran had done or who he was. I don't think I trust this Warren guy any more than you do, but he wasn't trying to hurt anyone else. He definitely wasn't the one firing in all directions: any of us could have been killed." She looked down at Sebastian. "And you don't even know who this is, do you?" He nodded, conceding the point. She said, "I need a pretty strong reason if I'm going to leave someone to bleed to death."

He could see she was making up her mind as she was speaking. Now she nodded to herself, the decision made. "I think we should go and see what happened to Warren. And we have to do what we can for this guy."

Clipper wasn't so sure. It seemed fairly likely to him that Warren was going to cause them both some real trouble soon enough. If Warren had killed Gary then he was absolutely ruthless, because Gary wouldn't have been a threat – he wouldn't have talked or caused trouble. What reason would anyone have for getting rid of him, except to shut him up permanently? If that was a reason to kill, then Warren obviously considered those around him disposable.

On the other hand, if Warren *was* now dead – if he'd fallen onto the rails along with Kieran – then Clipper wouldn't mind knowing that.

Slightly against his better judgement he said, "I suppose I should go and look. You can do more for this bloke than I can."

Rachel shook her head as if to say that what she could do for him wasn't that much – but she wasn't arguing with his suggestion. He stood, finding that he was still hunched over – it just seemed too weird not to duck down a little bit, what with all the shooting – but he forced himself to straighten up. He touched Rachel's shoulder, not exactly sure why, and give her the best smile he could manage, and then began moving towards the gaping door of the rear cab.

***

In that cramped driver's cab, Kieran hadn't had much time to think, but that was OK. He'd already done all the thinking he needed to do and made all the decisions he needed to make.

For Kieran, life had divided pretty neatly into two sections. There was his real life, the first one, where everything that happened was fairly normal – and occasionally exceptional – but it all tended to make about as much sense as anyone else's. And then there was the second part that followed, which was like something Kafka might have come up with if he'd been hungover and in a rush. This second life *seemed* real enough, but it was strangely twisted and the logic of it often eluded him. Some of the events just seemed to have squirmed their way out of an acid trip and into reality. Not that anyone seemed to do acid any more. But in Kieran's time it had been big.

He'd been pretty average as a child, though he was brighter than most, and he'd never had much time for rules. But he used his wits to get himself out of most trouble. He'd liked learning and he'd liked books. But he'd liked sex and drugs and rock'n'roll even more – though he'd always compartmentalised, and kept the two separate. And the former paid for the latter. His brains did the work, his body reaped the rewards – or at least felt the effects.

Even in his mid-teens he was insatiable when it came to new experiences, mixing with a much older crowd and often staying out all night. But no matter how much his leisure time was like something from the annals of the Hellfire Club he'd always made sure his studies didn't suffer.

Towards the end of the Seventies he was at university, attending lectures during the day, and by night living a life that would have blown the minds of his college friends. He was dealing to pay for it all, which is how he knew only too well when the Seventies really came to an end and the Eighties began. Even if you didn't know what year you were living in you could see the change in the way that the hash and the acid market dried up, and instead of selling tabs and bags of weed to hippies in Afghan coats he was selling a grand's worth of coke at a time to guys his own age who wore suits that cost more than his car – and drove cars that cost more than his flat. They looked like junior executives but they lived like the Borgias and for a while he found himself starting to get jealous. He was severely tempted to swap dealing for trading. But then he came to his senses.

He was halfway through a PhD in Economics and one day he was talking to a friend about the North Sea oil boom. His friend was explaining how the best place to be in a boom was in the second-tier. If the boom was a gold rush, you sold picks and shovels and mules. If the boom was offshore oil you sold underwater welding equipment or chartered out helicopters. There was less competition, you could charge what you liked and you could probably survive a downturn if you were smart.

That really resonated with Kieran, particularly as he was watching the financial boom of the Eighties get started. He'd been feeling like he had his nose pressed up against the window watching the party from outside in the cold. Right before his eyes, Wall Street and the City were waking up to all sorts of possibilities. They were getting a fetish for high-risk sex with the money markets: leveraged acquisitions, asset stripping, and kinky new ways to securitise or play fast-and-loose with bond issues. Simultaneously the government was flogging off public infrastructure like peddlers on Oxford Street unloading nicked jewellery. It had all the hallmarks of a boom with all the possibilities that entailed.

Kieran quickly forgot about changing jobs; he was better placed exactly where he was, he just had to make a few changes. If anyone managed to pull off the perfect Eighties hat-trick and asset-strip a recently-privatised utility while financing the deal with junk bonds, Kieran wanted to be right there to make sure the adrenaline-crazed twenty-eight-year-old in question was afforded all the appropriate luxuries, comforts and indulgences his ego-less id could desire.

Understanding the markets helped Kieran be in the right place at the right time, and when his customers got rich, so did he. Financially at least, the Eighties were very good to Kieran. By 1988 he owned two clubs and a boutique hotel on the edge of the City, both with members-only areas and private rooms and lots of security. He owned a very prestigious executive dining service that would deliver chilled champagne and fresh Cornish oysters right to your corner office – or whatever else you wanted: the menu was extensive, expensive and typically included little cloisonné boxes of powdered crystals as a side-dish. He also owned two dance studios and a PR firm. Both were legit, but any girls from the dance studios who wanted to earn extra cash could work nights for the PR firm wearing hot pants and draping themselves over new cars or handing out leaflets, whatever was required of them. And if any of the girls needed even more extra cash they could graduate to the third tier of that particular business enterprise – what Kieran euphemistically called 'executive hospitality'. It dovetailed beautifully with the other businesses, helped him make all the right contacts – and since Kieran's grasp of finance and accounting exceeded that of anyone in the City of London police force or Special Branch, the chances of him being caught were slimmer than a dance-studio drop-out on a cocaine-only diet.

Kieran was meticulously careful to maintain genuinely profitable and legitimate front companies for all of his lucrative *demi-monde* ventures – though sometimes reality could outstrip even his most optimistic expectations. For a while his ultra-high-end lunch service threatened to make more money than the drug dealing it was designed to conceal. It was what Kieran's lecturers would have called 'negative price elasticity': you put up your prices and that only increased the demand for your services because it made it clear to everyone on the sidelines that your clients were the real thing: vulgarly, profligately super-rich.

Logistically, financially and creatively the organisation he created was a roaring success. The one area he struggled in was security. In all other ways, every business was complementary to every other one: the girls, the clubs, the hotel, the drugs, the stratospherically priced dining service all overlapped; but security never seemed to fit. His clients wanted things easy, calm, hassle-free, low-key – but at the same time they wanted cast-iron, gold-plated security, so that no one – police, journalists or Kieran's rival entrepreneurs – could interfere. It was a difficult balancing act. So over the years he hired bouncers, martial artists, ex-policemen, working policemen, ex-army officers, disgraced CIA officers, avaricious KGB agents and out-and-out thugs, and still he never quite felt he'd got that side of things covered.

The fact was that every now and again he would brush up against another crime organisation – usually one much older, larger and nastier than his – and there'd be trouble. Often you didn't even know who you were dealing with; you just pulled back before you found out. He certainly didn't want to go head-to-head with anyone. The last thing he needed was shoot-outs and tit-for-tat killings with the Mafia or the Triads or the Yakuza or salt-of-the-earth East End villains. By spending a large slice of his turnover on security, and by constantly innovating his way into new markets, he managed to avoid coming to the attention of any of the big players. As a result, by 1990 he was a very rich man.

But as the Eighties waned, so did he. The change – what his lecturers would have called his personal 'inflection point' – was marked by two events, two signs that his fortunes had shifted. One was tiny, the other less so. The larger of the two was still rather on the slight side and took the form of a tall, slim woman with pale skin wearing a beautifully tailored suit who crippled two of Kieran's meatiest bouncers with an insouciance that was so total and so convincing that it actually made most of what she said to him afterwards seem plausible.

The second omen was far smaller. It was the virus Hepatitis B. Kieran had heard of it but he'd got the distinct impression it wasn't that bad, which for many people it wasn't. But in the years to follow he was to revise his initial view a number of times. To begin with, it took him a while to recognise that there was anything wrong with him, because all the symptoms – aches, persistent tiredness, nausea, headaches – were things he expected to feel anyway given the kinds of 'hobbies' he would pursue once he was done with the office for the day.

When he tried cutting back a little, taking a few nights off – even getting to bed before midnight on a couple of occasions – his health still didn't improve, so he went to see a doctor. That was the start of a whole era of visiting doctors, sitting in expensive waiting rooms with good art on the walls, being addressed by attractive receptionists with immaculate manners who still managed to be just as unwelcoming as the stressed-out old bats he remembered from when he was a kid waiting to see the family GP.

Initially he was told it was alcohol poisoning or 'substance abuse' or chronic fatigue. Reluctantly he began to cut back even more on his recreations. As his symptoms got worse he mounted ever more drastic incursions into the land of healthy living. After one very memorable six-week period in a 'celebrity retreat', during which he consumed nothing more exciting and harmful than camomile tea, his Harley Street specialist eventually concluded he had a chronic viral infection.

It was around this time he had his visit from the tall, pale, insanely-dangerous woman in the grey Donna Karan pinstripe. She didn't stay long, but she made him the most extraordinary proposal he had ever heard. She said she represented a group of people with pretty much unlimited reach and influence who, while they had no interest in working for a living, rather liked having money and power. She proposed that they take over the ownership of his business, though not its day-to-day running. He could remain in place, draw a handsome salary and give the lion's share of the profits to them.

While he was not an aggressive man, he hadn't grown wealthy living on the wrong side of the law by being soft. Whatever the truth of her claims, it didn't do for people to think you were a pushover. He squared up to her, ready to put on a show of righteous anger – all the while hoping that whoever was supposed to be watching the door downstairs still had enough unbroken fingers to dial a telephone and call in some reinforcements. But astonishingly he found he couldn't move, could hardly breathe. It was the first of many such surreal experiences, and while they never ceased to be troubling, he eventually began to accept them as emblematic of the less pleasant and more Kafkaesque second phase of his life.

With his breath stuck in his throat and the panic of suffocation beginning to flush blood to his cheeks he listened to her complete her proposal. She would be back to visit him in a week and he could do what he liked in the meantime. He could change his name and fly to South America, he could hire a mercenary army to protect him, he could call the police, or book himself on the next Space Shuttle flight. In one week's time she would return, she would kill or maim everyone who stood in her way, and she would expect him to shake her hand and accept that he now worked for her and the people she answered to.

It was actually the phrase 'the people she answered to' that bothered him the most: the idea that there was a hierarchy at work here and he wasn't even dealing with the top rung of it was heartily distressing.

In the intervening week he did his best, though sometimes it felt like he was just going through the motions. He found an old sea fort on the Norfolk coast that had been retrofitted with a fall-out shelter in the late Seventies and he locked himself in there. He hired half a dozen freelance Israeli snipers to patrol the ramparts and borrowed a security team from a supplier of his in the Shan States: men who were usually deployed guarding drug convoys and fighting off honest-to-god pirates in the South China Sea. It didn't do him much good, as some part of him knew it wouldn't.

His one consolation, looking back on it, was that the tall, pale woman – whose name was Karst – had needed some assistance in getting to him. It was slim consolation indeed because her 'team' had consisted of one other, a young woman who only looked to be about seventeen according to one of the snipers who'd survived. While Kieran never got to know Karst very well, he did have occasional insights into her thinking. She was nothing if not calculating. With hindsight he suspected the young woman she'd brought with her would have been selected largely for psychological effect. Karst had made sure to kick his ass with what his male chauvinism would have to assume was their 'B' team. She'd leave it to him to imagine what a team made up of half a dozen of their alpha males was capable of.

For a while, working for Karst was actually a pleasant surprise – not because it was a bundle of laughs, but because his expectations had been so very low. He really was allowed to carry on pretty much as before, with the obvious proviso that three-quarters of the profits now went to someone else. He also had to submit to random inspections by their accountant, who was a strange man: frightened for his life much of the time and yet living like a king on the salary they paid him.

After three months, Karst came to see him in person for a second time. She explained that the next day she was going to come back and break his left arm. He protested that he had done nothing wrong and that he'd obeyed every order he'd been given. She said she knew that, and that was why it was only an arm – that and the fact he had a low psychological tolerance for physical harm. She lingered long enough to give him a brief lecture on the psychology of intimidation.

You had to be careful with proud men, she said, because hurting them could be counter-productive. It was usually best to attack their sense of control over their environment, perhaps by hurting a family member. In Kieran's case, she said his pride was intellectual and hurting him physically would work perfectly well as a motivator, with the proviso that he must always be given a chance to protect himself first. This, she explained, would make it clear that he couldn't think his way out of the situation, no matter how cleverly he schemed. That, plus the fear of more pain, would ensure he didn't start looking for a way to regain his independence. She had selected the three-month mark because it was the time at which a sense of normality started to set in, and with it a possible resurgence of confidence, and thus it was a good moment to reinforce the lessons of their first encounter.

"Really," she stressed, "it's good that you fear pain and the prospect of being physically mutilated. If you didn't, I might have to do something far, far worse than break a single bone."

She turned to go and then remembered something: "Oh, and no painkillers. I'll take a blood sample tomorrow. If your blood contains anything I don't approve of we'll have to go through this again, and next time I'll be creative. That isn't something you'd enjoy."

He didn't sleep much that night, as no doubt she'd intended. The expectation was far worse than the event, which was still bad enough to give him nightmares afterwards. He just wasn't the sort of person who could take pain in his stride, not to mention the sensation of a bone snapping. And despite the fact that he would remember that experience as long as he lived, Karst had found a way to make it even more memorable. She had caught him in whatever invisible net she'd used to cut off his breath the first time they'd met and then she'd reached out towards him, not even making contact, and he'd felt his left humerus break.

As she left him with tears rolling down his face she gave him one last piece of wisdom, "Think about this too. I've never lied to you. When I tell you something will happen, it happens. That's important, because one day I will promise you something good and I want you to know that it's guaranteed, just like any of the painful things I predict for you. One day I'll tell you how you can retire in comfort. It will be something to look forward to. But it won't be for a while yet."

The 'good thing' she'd mentioned was a long time in coming, but eventually it did arrive. First Kieran had to go through most of a decade of despair and agony. The effects of the hepatitis grew worse. No treatment worked; he was one of the fraction of the population whose immune systems couldn't defeat the infection. Eventually it turned into cirrhosis. Which then progressed to a viral form of liver cancer.

Until it got really bad, Kieran carried on working. Even when he was spending most of his day lying helpless in an electrically-adjustable hospital bed he still got a kick out of directing the business – as Karst knew he would. It distracted him from the fact that he was dying. And of course since Karst's takeover, he never needed to worry about security any more. If someone caused him problems he had a number he could call and that was that.

As his condition grew worse it became clear that he needed a new liver. And even though they'd fudged his medical records to make him appear more eligible than he was, he'd still been on the waiting list for three years and no suitable donor had presented themselves. He couldn't wait much longer. And so in '94 he had his transplant; it took place in Costa Rica and Karst's people arranged everything. He didn't ask where the liver had come from or whether the donor had finished with it before it was extracted.

But rather than restore his health, the transplant brought with it a new set of problems. Tissue rejection set in, and the drugs he took to control his rebellious immune system allowed other infections to blossom. For eleven months he was more or less in a coma, getting weaker every day.

Time passed in a blur. And then one day he woke up. For a while he thought he'd died. He was dressed in white, in a beautiful room looking out over the mountains of Tuscany and he felt so healthy he thought he might burst. One look in the mirror convinced him that this must be some form of afterlife. His reflection showed a man in his late teens or perhaps the start of his twenties, whereas Kieran had just turned forty. The face he saw was his, though – except that his nose was different. Kieran's nose had been big and bent; now it was straight and rather average.

The sense that he was in heaven lasted for the rest of that day and into the evening. And then, as he watched the sun setting over the distant peaks, Karst came to see him to explain what had happened, and he realised he was still alive.

She said, "We consider this an honour. We have made you young and healthy, which is not something we would normally do for... an employee. I told you one day that I would make you a promise and that it would be something good. This is the beginning of it. Saving your life is a reward for what you have done for us up until now."

She gave him a moment to let that sink in and then went on, "We want you to go back to work. In fact, we want you to take on some extra responsibilities. You're an ideal choice to run several of our operations and I think you'll enjoy the challenges of your new job."

Kieran sensed there was a 'but' coming. This definitely wasn't heaven: no afterlife he'd ever imagined would have included working for Karst. This seemed a lot more like business as usual, but taken to a new level of weirdness.

Karst said, "We're good employers. The longer you work for us the better your retirement package will be, but we can offer you one thing no one else can. We'll give you back all the years that you give to us. When you leave us, you'll be young and rich and free. But first you have to earn it. Does that sound fair?"

Karst had him pegged. By now he knew that crossing her was certain death – and doubtless dramatically excruciating. This latest development proved that if they wanted to they could ensure that working for them cost him nothing and gained him everything. It really was an offer you couldn't refuse.

As she was leaving, Karst mentioned, "We threw in an old-fashioned nose job for free. It avoids various complications down the line."

Like having anyone believe his story if he chose to tell someone, he thought. His fingerprints weren't on record anywhere, he'd always maintained a low profile, he had no proper longstanding friendships or any living relatives he was in touch with – and he didn't even look like the old Kieran. He smiled in cold appreciation; Karst really knew her stuff.

It took a while for the reality of the change to sink in. His first job was to rebuild the top level of his old organisation, replacing anyone who'd known him before. The parts of the business that had been on the downturn in the early Nineties were on their last legs by now. It was time for a fresh start. Karst gave him control of a number of additional ventures she'd previously been handling directly. He was able to make himself useful by bringing his usual flair for synergy and clever logistics to each of them. As Karst had promised, he even enjoyed it for a little while. But then his curiosity began to stir and threatened to spoil it for him.

He would occasionally meet Karst's colleagues and found them to be as taciturn as she was. More so in fact, because Karst would sometimes give these little illustrative lectures aimed at realigning the sensibilities and motivations of her direct reports, whereas the others paid no attention to him at all.

Despite the danger, Kieran found himself trying to learn more about who these people were and how they were able to do the remarkable things they could do. From time to time he would see evidence of their strange abilities which, breathtaking though they were, certainly had limits.

Unfortunately for him, Karst eventually became aware of his interest and decided to give him another corrective lesson. But first, as always, she wanted to explain.

"You need to understand that my ability to manipulate you psychologically is what keeps you alive. If we ever reach the point where I can think of no way to make you do what I want, then your usefulness would be gone. That fact underlies any other deal we might have in operation."

She gave him a kind of moonlit smile and said, "Your intellectual curiosity is valuable to your work, but if I come to believe that work alone is not enough to occupy your thoughts we will have reached an impasse. And I only know one method for resolving those."

She continued, "You have the whole wide world to distract yourself with and a surfeit of professional challenges. Unless you can redirect the curiosity you feel in some new direction, I will be forced to replace you."

Kieran was doing his best to listen to her, but by now he was also aware that the talking part of the lesson would soon be over and the hurting him and breaking things part might be about to start.

But a thought occurred to Karst and she said in a voice that was almost kindly, "It might interest you to know that I was born a very long time ago, and believe it or not I once had a mother. There was a piece of advice she would sometimes give to people. It doesn't translate very poetically, but let me try: it was something along the lines of 'why study power when you can study happiness instead?'. I have never been able to do much with it, but perhaps you will. I think if you can take it to heart, it could save your life."

And then instead of hurting him or issuing some terrible prediction about what would happen a day or a week later, she drove him to one of their buildings in the City and locked him in its ancient cellar. She left him there in total darkness to 'give him some time to think about the nature of curiosity' and to 'make pacts with himself about how he would behave if she ever let him out'. Previously, she had fought his defiance by combining fear and pain; now she fought his curiosity by mixing fear with sensory deprivation.

Nearly two days had passed when she finally returned to release him. And he did indeed find that his curiosity was much lessened for a time, wonderfully so in fact. In that cellar, with absolutely nothing to focus on except his own thoughts, he'd done just as she'd expected and come to wholeheartedly regret his inquisitiveness. She had more or less cured him of his curiosity.

And perhaps things would have stayed that way if he hadn't met someone who offered him a way out from under Karst's control.

The fact was that Kieran was no longer happy. In fact, at his core, he was miserable. But the impossibility of escape and an appreciation for just how perceptive Karst could be kept him from acting on it. The problem was that he had changed. His old pleasures didn't satisfy him any more and he found himself gradually giving them up, only indulging himself sufficiently to stop Karst suspecting some fresh shift in his character which might lead her to look for new torments with which to manipulate him. He thought wryly to himself that perhaps he was just getting old. He was nearing his fiftieth birthday, feeling like he was ninety, while the face he saw in the mirror could certainly pass for late twenties.

The way out he was offered came from one of Karst's colleagues. Much as she would have done, he first made it clear how easy it would be to reciprocate if Kieran betrayed him. Then he explained that, much like Kieran, he wanted some independence. But before he could strike out on his own, he needed to get his hands on one or two of life's little comforts to make sure that his voluntary exile was as agreeable as possible. For this he needed information. Kieran wouldn't need to physically do anything. He'd simply need to compile a picture of the operations which he supervised and then hand that information over. In exchange, he would receive a lump sum of two hundred thousand U.S. dollars in cash and a chance to start over, with Karst and her friends thinking he was dead.

Once upon a time, two hundred grand U.S. would have meant very little, but these days his access to funds was severely restricted. Karst let him have almost anything he wanted, but someone else always paid; he had very little discretionary cash of his own. Unless he wanted to risk getting caught, then squirrelling away even fifty thousand pounds would be a struggle. Given his increasingly frugal tastes, two hundred grand would be enough. In fact, to his surprise, he realised he would have done it for no money at all; his freedom was what he really wanted.

Still it took him two months to work up the nerve to say yes – even though from the moment he heard the offer he knew he had to take it. It was just that crossing Karst was not something you did on the spur of the moment. In fact he'd come to think of it as playing Russian roulette with a fully loaded gun.

He never learned very much about the identity of the man who made him the offer, beyond the initial he used to identify himself: 'J'. Over the course of six months Kieran copied all sorts of data for him: e-mails, bank records, property transactions, travel information. Kieran was administering a large organisation, and while he often didn't know what purpose its activities served he was still in a position to record many of them.

He did his best to give no clue to Karst that anything had changed. But inside, he was the happiest he had been for a very long time. Though it hadn't had quite the effect she intended, he had found the advice Karst had passed on from her long-dead mother surprising memorable. It really resonated with him. So much so that he had had it engraved on a little silver card that he kept in his wallet. It had taken him a long time to get there, but he felt as though he might actually be ready to start enjoying the simple things in life.

As the time approached for him to hand over the information, and undergo his fake death, it even looked like he was going to get away with it. In the end, he never found out what had given the game away, but a full day ahead of schedule he got a call from J telling him to bring what he'd got right that second because someone was on to them.

"This will still work,' J told him, "They don't know that I'm involved. I can still cover your tracks when you disappear. In fact, this might make things easier."

They met in the big train station at Stratford in East London. J handed over a backpack full of bundles of hundred dollar bills; Kieran handed over two data CDs packed with files. He knew J would only need to pick up the phone and his life was over, but he also knew it would be difficult for him to do so without incriminating himself. Just to make things even more secure, Kieran had a second pair of discs in his old briefcase and they contained some extra files he hadn't given to J, including a couple of e-mails they'd exchanged. It wouldn't necessarily keep him safe – unless J anticipated something like this – but it *would* make it just that bit more difficult for J to get away with it, if he double-crossed Kieran.

When the exchange was complete, Kieran walked away from J with the beginnings of an irrepressible smile spreading across his face. He found a gents toilets, shut himself into a cubicle and transferred the cash into his old briefcase, wrapping two bundles of notes in cling-film and slipping them in alongside a 9mm semi-automatic and a fake passport, both of which he'd owned since before Karst had come onto the scene. Then he changed into clothes he'd bought in a charity shop, putting his

Armani suit in the bag J had given him, and dropping that into a litter bin near the station. Then he boarded a Jubilee Line train for Canary Wharf, where he would pick up the rest of his things and get a taxi to City Airport. At that moment, he allowed himself to believe it was going to work.

And he very nearly made it. He was getting off the tube train, when the young man in the cheap suit came pelting towards him with someone chasing after him and Kieran realised that his one chance of freedom had slipped away. They'd sent a couple faces he wouldn't recognise and dressed them as police, but he instantly saw them for what they were. Very few ordinary people moved the way they did. You needed to be young for a lot of years to acquire that murderous grace. His spirits were in free-fall.

Dressing them as some sort of police SWAT team was a nice touch. Ideal if you wanted to haul someone away in broad daylight with no questions asked. No other criminal organisation would even dare to try something like that, but he knew that Karst's people could call on some astonishingly illustrious official connections if they needed to. Not that they'd probably have bothered; none of their kind would worry about being captured or questioned. They could break through any cordon, resist any attempts to contain them. Short of calling in the army, they were unstoppable.

So it seemed like Kieran was going to be captured and dragged back to Karst. Then she would want to know who he'd been working with. If he was lucky she would just kill him once he talked. But knowing Karst, she might decide to use him as an object lesson to her other direct reports. That was enough to turn your stomach, just thinking about it. Very soon now, he was going to die – one way or another – that was pretty much a certainty. And he found that finality lent him a certain determination, almost like courage, that he hadn't experienced before. The fact was that if he decided that he wouldn't allow himself to be hauled back to face Karst then that was all there was to it. He would find a way out whatever the cost. It was all he really wanted now anyway: to be free.

***

Clipper stood at the entrance to the rear cab and looked outwards towards the dark track. Light from behind him illuminated part of the dim interior and a little of the tunnel beyond. He could see that one of the train's rear windows was missing. Presumably that was the result of the gunshot he'd heard just after Warren cornered Kieran in here.

The outer door of the train lay open as well. It hinged, not along its side like a normal door, but along its bottom edge, which meant that it opened like a drawbridge – though this drawbridge had steps built into it and formed a descending ramp down to the level of the tracks. Plastic-wrapped steel cables ran out from the sides of the doorframe and down to the ramp, holding it at the proper angle. Sitting on the bottom step, legs dangling over the tracks, was Warren.

Clipper's eyes adjusted gradually to the gloom. A slight stirring of air in the tunnel brought to him the smell of dust and hot oil and… with a nauseating jolt he realised what that third smell might be and did his best not to think about it.

Once his eyes had got used to the low light, he could make out what Warren was doing. He had one arm raised and was gently flicking his right hand out in front of him and then slowly rolling his arm in a circle around his shoulder.

"Er… Are you OK?" Clipper asked, not sure what to make of it, but feeling as though he should say something to announce his presence. He'd been really hoping that Warren hadn't survived, that he'd fallen along with Kieran, so it felt strange to be asking him how he was doing. On the other hand, he'd seen no sign that these people could read minds, so he did his best to keep the guilt to himself.

Warren's tone was biting as he said, "Well, you see I pulled my shoulder out of its socket. It's still a little painful."

Presumably he'd tried to grab hold of Kieran as he jumped; Clipper could work that much out. But how had he *un*-dislocated his shoulder? He could vaguely remember tough guys in movies charging into walls to pop them back in. He wasn't sure he believed that would work. Still, if you could deflect bullets and stop yourself from bleeding through force of will, the shoulder thing was probably kid's stuff. Child's play. A doddle.

Was that a little hysteria creeping into his thoughts? Clipper took a breath and tried to settle himself. Warren still hadn't looked round as

Clipper said, "I'm sorry but your, uh… your friend isn't doing very well. We don't know what else to do for him."

Warren sighed and began to haul himself to his feet. He still had on only one boot and Clipper could just about make out the black mark in the middle of his bare foot that must have been the clotted blood around the bullet hole. There was no sign of bleeding. Warren was even able to put a little weight on it as he stood.

Once he was upright he said, "Well, try not to concern yourself." More sarcasm? He grunted a little as he turned, his bad arm holding onto one of the ramp's steel cables. "I think Sebastian is going to have to chalk this one up to experience." His tone was conversational now – he was mainly talking to himself – and yet there was something troubling about his words.

Clipper edged back as Warren limped towards him. Wanting to get out of his way, Clipper turned and walked ahead, making his way back to Rachel's side. When Warren eventually reached them, he crouched down next to Sebastian, glaring at Rachel until she moved aside to give him some room. Then he gently touched his friend's face and called his name. Getting no response, he said it again and patted his cheek to rouse him. Still no response. A look of annoyance passed crossed Warren's features. He lifted his hand a little and gave Sebastian a hard slap across the face. Rachel gasped.

Irate, she demanded, "What the hell do you think you're…" but then she abruptly stopped speaking. Clipper couldn't figure out what was happening now, but Rachel's eyes bulged a little and there was a look of panic on her face. Her mouth was open but so far as he could tell she wasn't breathing.

When Rachel had challenged him, Warren's head had snapped round to stare at her and his eyes were still fixed upon her now as she squirmed and struggled to breathe. It was plain enough that Warren was doing this. Somehow.

Clipper needed to do something to help Rachel, but he had no idea what. Several options flicked through his mind, and all of them seemed likely to make matters worse – especially his first instinct, which was just to punch Warren in the face.

He realised he needed to say something to distract Warren and maybe get him to calm down a little, but all that Clipper's throat wanted to produce was a shout of anger. And that wasn't going to work.

He forced himself to sound calm as he said, "Hey, listen, she was only trying to help your friend, alright? That's fair enough isn't it?" He needed to sound reasonable, not like he was challenging Warren, but it wasn't easy.

A moment later Rachel dragged in a great lungful of air and Warren said to her, "Keep your mouth shut." Then he turned back to Sebastian, whose eyes had fluttered open. He was clearly having difficulty focusing on the man leaning over him. Clipper could almost see him trying to figure out whether someone had just hit him. It didn't look like his brain was firing on all cylinders.

"Here, look at me, Sebastian," Warren said, clicking his fingers and trying to get his attention. Then, very clearly and emphatically, he said, "You need to stop the bleeding right now. Right now, understand?" Sebastian said nothing, though he looked as though he was trying to speak. Then his eyes began to flick upwards again and the lids closed.

This time when Warren hit him, even harder than before, Rachel tensed and Clipper could see how tightly her nails pressed into the palms of her bunched fists, but she held her tongue.

Sebastian twitched and quivered from the blow, but his eyes opened once more. Warren said to him, "This is it, my friend. If you're going to save yourself you need to do it now."

Sebastian coughed a little, deep down in his chest, hardly making a sound and his lips moved, but all that came out was a wheeze. He tried again and managed to say, "It's no good. I can't maintain it…" He snatched another couple of painful sounding breaths and went on, "Hospital. Let them fix me up. I'll get out… when I'm stronger."

But Warren was shaking his head slowly. He sounded sad as he said, "Sebastian, that isn't how it works. You know the rules. You'd get us a lot of attention. And they'd take away these." He tapped Sebastian's wrist as he said it.

Sebastian looked confused and then just a little bit worried. "No. I can… Give me a moment…" he said, struggling to speak.

Warren shook his head again. Then he reached around and pulled a black tube free from the bottom of his backpack. Clipper tried to figure out what it was, but couldn't guess. Warren grasped it at either end and pulled his hands apart. A bright knife-edge came into view. It was a blade about eight inches long. Sebastian's eyes went very wide and he began struggling to move, but his arms had no strength in them, they did little more than flutter at his sides.

"No," Rachel said sharply. And when Warren shot her a warning look, she held her hands to her mouth and repeated quietly, "No," but she didn't try to stop him.

For Clipper it was like the moment when he'd seen Kieran hanging from the rear of the train. His mind raced – aware of what was going to happen next, but unable to think of a way to prevent it.

"Couldn't we…" he began, not caring if Warren turned on him. But Warren had already done it. He'd rested the tip of the knife on Sebastian's chest and pushed the blade in between his ribs. Sebastian twitched once, violently and made a sound that was halfway between a moan and a cough, and that was that. Clipper could hardly believe that was all it took to kill someone.

Warren waited a few seconds and then eased the blade out. He gave his wrist a violent twist which cast a line of blood droplets in a thin arc up onto the white of the door panel and then he shut the knife back into its sheath with a snap. He used his sleeve to wipe the handle free of his fingerprints and then tucked the sheathed knife into Sebastian's belt.

Since the moment she'd seen the mirrored steel exposed and realised what it meant, Rachel had been staring at Warren with fixed and silent hatred. Her gaze burrowed into him and Clipper thought he would surely be forced to look round in a minute, to react. Mentally Clipper pleaded with her to stop before she attracted Warren's attention and he was provoked into doing something awful to her. Given what he'd just seen Warren do, Clipper could picture it so easily: Rachel's body crumpling, her life extinguished, while Clipper looked on helplessly.

But Warren was busying himself with Sebastian's personal effects. He was removing the fastenings around Sebastian's wrists. One was a watch; Clipper wasn't sure what the strap on the other wrist was for. He also removed Sebastian's wool cap and a bright band of metal beneath it. It looked out of place next to the black uniform.

Was this what gave them their power, Clipper wondered. Was this like those stories where people had magic rings or wands and stuff? Or could it be some sort of technology, some kind of miniaturised gadgetry – perhaps secret military equipment beyond anything civilians had access to? He had no idea. For all Clipper could tell the things Warren was removing might simply be their equivalent of dog tags – or taking a man's wedding ring back for his widow.

Now Warren turned Sebastian's body onto its side – and despite the fact that moments before he'd ended the man's life, he was gentle about it. He opened Sebastian's backpack and removed a few objects, some of which Clipper could identify – like a wallet and a phone – and some he could only guess at, like the black tube that resembled Warren's knife but was much longer. Then he worked his way along Sebastian's corpse, expertly rifling the body and removing everything that could be removed. When he was done, he slipped his own backpack off and stowed Sebastian's things, and then shrugged it back into place.

When his task was completed he half stood, bending down to get his hands beneath Sebastian's body, and lifted it off the floor. Moving slowly and favouring his good foot, he carried the body past Clipper and Rachel, and took it into the rear cab, placing it on the floor behind the driver's chair. As Warren stepped back from the body, Clipper could see him pulling his sleeve down over his hand, before he bent down again. When he straightened he was holding the knife in the fabric of his tunic. He flicked his arm and the knife spun away into the dark of the tunnel. He must have loosened the scabbard too, for Clipper saw a flash as the blade caught the light. He could hear it clatter and ring as it bounced across the tracks. He wondered whether Kieran wasn't going to get the blame for the hole in Sebastian's chest as well as the one in his neck.

Now what? Clipper thought, ominously aware that there was nothing left to occupy Warren's attention apart from him and Rachel – and so far the recipients of Warren's attention hadn't lasted very long. But there wasn't any reason for him to hurt them, was there?

The problem was that Clipper just didn't know how to read someone like Warren – and that frustrated as well as frightened him. He'd been around some dangerous people, but you could usually tell when you were in trouble with them. They tended to shout a lot and threaten you, and they made it pretty clear when they were getting ready to do something physical. But who could work out what was going on in Warren's head? Should Clipper assume he was safe for the time being – at least until

Warren got out another knife? Or should he be freaking out right now and sprinting for the other end of the train? Which just seemed guaranteed to force Warren's hand and make him do something unpleasant.

He looked over at Rachel to see how she was doing, and noticed tears in her eyes. She was looking towards the cab – to where Sebastian's body lay – and he realised she was crying for the man who had been killed, and the fact that she hadn't been able to save him – and that made Clipper feel worthless and low. He was busy worrying about his own safety while she was wishing she could have done more to help an injured man. He felt a wave of disgust with himself. This situation was just bringing home to him what he'd been feeling for a while now: he was a parasite who always put himself first.

He just hoped he could hide that from Rachel for a little bit longer. They were in a lot of trouble here, but it sort of felt like they were a team. And that was so much better than going through this on his own. Which meant he desperately didn't want her to notice what a self-centred loser he was.

Dammit, he was doing it again: turning it around so it was about him. He was going to think about somebody else's wellbeing for a change before his self-esteem just shrivelled up and blew away.

He reached out to touch Rachel's arm and said quietly, "It'll be OK." He wasn't sure *what* would be OK – it didn't seem likely that anything very much would be – but that wasn't exactly the point.

Rachel looked up at him, and he tried to think of something else to say that would help her to feel better. "You really tried," he said, and he meant it. "You didn't know him, but you still did everything you could for him."

She didn't respond to that, but after a few moments she nodded a little and he reckoned that maybe he'd consoled her a little. Neither of them spoke for a few seconds, until Rachel lifted her head and said, "I think you were right about him." She meant Warren. "We should have just run."

Well, he wasn't going to get into that line of thought. And sadly, he couldn't change the subject by explaining his genius plan to get them out of there because he didn't have one. In fact there wasn't really anything useful he could do, unless it was just to distract her a little. He said, "You know, I really would like to see those horses you mentioned. I'm just a bit worried your mum won't take to me. She sounds like she can be awkward when she wants to be."

Rachel give a single laugh and said, "Well if *that's* all that's spoiling your day, I can tell you now, there's *no way* she'll approve. But you shouldn't let that put you off visiting. She hates it when people give up too easily." She didn't really smile, but she looked at him in a way that made him feel like they'd just shared a joke, which was what he'd wanted.

When Warren reappeared a moment later, Clipper felt like he'd been caught doing something he shouldn't have been, though he wasn't sure what. As Warren clumped towards them, passing between opposing rows of seats, he called out to them, "So what's the story with you two? Friends? Co-workers?"

Before he even thought about it, Clipper said, "She's my girlfriend." He sounded defiant and realised immediately it was kind of an idiotic thing to say. But he felt like he needed to put up some form of resistance, to obstruct Warren in some way, even if he didn't dare challenge him properly. Lying to him felt like a start; a small sign of independence. Plus, he couldn't help feeling a little protective towards Rachel. He wasn't exactly the expert, but out of the two of them, he had to imagine he'd spent more time around violent criminals than she had.

"Girlfriend? I doubt that," said Warren, "but you clearly know each other." Then he suddenly held his hands up, like he was making a big announcement, and said, "But listen, here's the good news. I only need one of you. Right? So you can go if you want. I just need her to stay." He sounded easygoing, but his eyes never left Clipper as he spoke.

When Clipper didn't react, Warren said, "I mean it. You can go. Get to the other end of the train with all the other passengers. If you get asked to describe me later, make sure you do a bad job of it and we'll be fine."

Clipper was looking from Warren's face to Rachel's. Warren was doing that trustworthy thing again, spreading his hands a little, trying to sound reasonable, even a little bit amiable. Rachel on the other hand now had a sharp look of fear in her eyes. It was evidently dawning on her that, bad as this situation was, there were ways in which it could get a lot worse.

"I…" Clipper said, not sure of what he was going to say. It was only a matter of time before Warren remembered why Clipper's face might be familiar, wasn't it? And if things turned ugly, what was the sense in both him *and* Rachel getting hurt?

Clipper half expected Rachel to say something, to demand that he stay, to make some sort of protest. Maybe even to beg him. But she didn't. She was making it easy for him; she was even avoiding his gaze. He studied her face trying to understand what she was thinking. She looked like she was working hard to keep the fear under control and... something else.

"Well?" said Warren.

But Clipper was still wanted to understand Rachel's expression. Somehow it mattered. It was clear that Warren's decision to split them up – and to let him go – had dropped the floor out from underneath her, but there was something else going on in her eyes besides fear. There was a struggle taking place. And then she spoke, quietly. "It'll be OK," she whispered. She was giving him permission to go, but her eyes were fixed upon her hands, which rested in her lap.

So that was it. He could read her expression now. She was struggling to persuade herself that she'd be fine on her own. She was clearly terrified, but she wasn't going to drag this out. That's why she wouldn't look at him or beg him. In her mind, he was already walking away, and she was doing her best to prepare for whatever happened next. She must know what Clipper would be thinking: that no one in their right mind would turn down Warren's offer of freedom just to keep a stranger company. He wondered, if things were the other way round, whether she would choose to stay. Well, she'd already decided against leaving him once. And now she was making it easy for him to walk away from her.

As always happened when he got stressed over some sort of decision, he found himself wishing he could ask Gary what to do. Of course Gary had never given him any advice for a situation like this. But he had once said something about nicking from people who might not be able to afford it. He'd told Clipper, "Don't do anything you'll hate yourself for. It's not worth it." And that was clear enough. Clipper wanted so badly *not* to be the kind of person who'd leave Rachel behind. He didn't want to despise himself; in fact he was desperate for a reason not to.

"I... don't want to leave without Rachel," Clipper said. He felt he should give a reason, but he wasn't about to launch into some crazy speech about his self-esteem. "You know how it is," was the best he could manage.

Warren studied him. "You're sure?" he asked. He was like one of those game-show hosts who tried to get you to change your mind the whole time, to make the game more fun for the audience. Clipper nodded.

And finally Rachel looked at him. He wasn't quite sure what the look signified – it certainly wasn't anything as straightforward as gratitude or relief. But at least she could look at him again. And he realised how much that meant to him.

"Excellent," said Warren. "I was hoping you'd say that because I've got a job for you. And we need to make a start before someone tries to get this train moving again and I'm forced to do something about that."

Clipper didn't know how to react. Warren had a job for him? So what was all that about letting him go? Clipper had felt nauseous but sort of noble about his decision to stay for all of maybe three seconds, but now the situation had shifted again.

"You see, someone has to go down that tunnel and get Kieran's things," Warren explained. "For the time being, I'm having one or two mobility issues. So, um, *Matt*? Why don't you go for me and I'll stay here with… Rachel wasn't it? I'll look after her until you come back." Warren laid his hand on Rachel's shoulder, his fingers towards her neck – the fingertips were hidden inside the tumble of her hair. The gesture was both protective and unpleasantly intimate. Rachel looked like she wanted to pull away from him, but she didn't.

Clipper didn't need it spelled out: he knew how a protection racket worked. If Warren didn't get what he wanted, he'd stop 'looking after' Rachel. Earlier, he'd just been testing Clipper to see whether he was prepared to give up a chance to escape for Rachel's sake – and Clipper had passed. Or failed, depending on how you looked at it. Effectively he'd just volunteered Rachel to be his leverage.

It reminded Clipper of chess. In movies, whenever two people got into this cat-and-mouse stuff, someone would point out it was like game of chess. Well, Clipper hated chess. He'd tried it two or three times and couldn't make any sense of it. The rules seemed like they were plucked out of thin air, and any time you thought you'd worked out what you were supposed to do next it just meant you were about to fall into a trap. This entire thing was *exactly* like chess and he hated it.

And besides all the mind games, Warren wanted him to go out into the tunnel. Well, the more he thought about that, the more he wasn't too thrilled about the idea of being down there on the tracks. He also didn't like to think about what state Kieran's body might be in. It had been bad enough standing by the back door of the train and smelling something that shouldn't be familiar but somehow was: a combination of burnt hair and overcooked barbeque meat. He tried not to picture what was waiting for him in the dark of the tunnel.

"What if the current is still on?" Clipper asked. He knew the trogs called it 'traction current'; and if it was on it meant that the live rail could kill you.

Warren smiled unpleasantly. "Work something out," he said. "Maybe you could just be careful what you touch."

Clipper was trying to remember what else he knew about underground trains besides the words 'traction current'. He knew one of the reasons the door on the back of the train folded down to make a set of steps was to evacuate passengers if something went wrong. And obviously London Underground didn't want people to be electrocuted as soon as they stepped off the ramp. Yeah, that was it: there was a locker full of emergency bits and pieces in the cab somewhere. He was trying to think what the item he needed was called. His brain kept insisting it was a JCB, but he knew that wasn't it. Then he had it: an SCD. Short circuit device. It was like a long clamp that fitted across the rails. He'd never seen one, but he knew about them. If the electricity came on, the SCD sent it straight into the other rails and sort of blew the fuse.

Clipper was nodding reluctantly now. "OK. I know there's a gadget in the cab we can use to make sure the power stays off," Clipper said, "I just need a bit of rope maybe. To lower it onto the track."

Warren looked at him questioningly.

Clipper said, "Look I'll do what you say, but I'm not going to dab my finger against the live rail to see if it's on. There should be a short-circuit thing in the driver's cab and then we just need a way to lower it down so that I can tell whether the juice is on or not."

"Fair enough," Warren said, sounding impatient. "Get your short-circuit whatever-it-is. I've got some line here." He slipped his backpack off and unzipped one of the compartments. Reaching in, he pulled out a bunched coil of black rope. It was no thicker than clothesline, but it had an expensive satiny sheen to it that suggested it might be a lot stronger than clothesline, maybe some kind of superfibre.

Warren undid the coil of rope and produced a metal multi-tool gadget from one of his pockets. He thumbed open a wicked looking knife blade and held it up.

"How much line do you need," Warren asked. As he spoke, the tip of the knife drifted close to Rachel's face; it was almost absentminded, but Clipper was sure it was intentional. All part of helping Clipper picture what would happen if he legged it away down the tunnel instead of doing as he was told.

"I dunno, about ten feet," Clipper said. And then an idea like a snap of static electricity popped into his head. Bam. There it was.

It was more than a little bit crazy and right away he wondered whether he should forget about it. On the other hand, there was a chance it would work.

Warren was parcelling out the rope, getting ready to cut it, and waving the knife around near Rachel's skin. That clinched it in Clipper's mind. He didn't have to go through with his idea, he just had to set it up. He might need something up his sleeve if things with Warren really turned bad.

Half distracted, trying to think it through, Clipper said, "Nah, don't worry about cutting it." He reached out and Warren shrugged and handed him the rope.

Clipper was putting the steps together in his mind, ticking off the order of events.

"What's so funny?" Warren asked suspiciously. "Are you high or something?"

Clipper realised he'd been smiling. The idea that was even now unfolding itself in his brain had originally come from something Gary had said. It felt like one last gift from his old buddy, exactly when he needed it most. And that had made him smile.

"No," said Clipper, "It's just been a strange day, you know?" Warren gave him a look that suggested he thought Clipper was insane.

Setting the rope down on the seat nearest him, Clipper said, "Let me get the short circuit thing." He walked away from Warren and into the dim cab. As soon as he stepped into the gloom he started violently, having forgotten that Sebastian's corpse was waiting in there, leaning against the wall in the dark, legs out in front of him, staring into forever.

Doing his best to ignore the dead man's gaze he looked around for anything that might be an equipment locker. It was easy enough to find; he undid the lock and opened the hinged cover. Inside he could see a shovel and an ice scraper, a folded tarpaulin and a long complicated looking metal rod that had to be the SCD. He wrestled it free of its clips and closed the cover.

The idea that had popped into his head a moment before was still there, occupying part of his attention, and as it assembled itself he was able to see it from different sides. At that very moment, he spotted a problem and just as quickly realised the answer. Before he could change his mind, he set the SCD aside and crouched over Sebastian's corpse. He'd just watched Warren fetch out a bundle of rope from his backpack. As swiftly as he could, he checked the same compartment in Sebastian's pack… and came up with an identical bundle of silky futuristic-looking line. Hastily he tossed it out onto the track, throwing it as far as he could and hoping that Warren wasn't watching. Then he tried to prop Sebastian's corpse back up, so that it was just as Warren had left it. Arranging the heavy limbs felt horribly wrong and Clipper had to avoid looking at the dead face or brushing against any bare skin. He did the best he could and left it. Then he grabbed the SCD and stepped back into the passenger compartment.

Warren was closer now that he had been; probably coming to investigate. Clipper held up the metal device and picked up the rope.

"You any good at knots?" Warren asked, sceptically.

Clipper knew a few. Like he'd told Rachel, he'd worked at a stables for a little while. You couldn't be around horses for long and not learn a bit about tying a knot. He shrugged noncommittally.

Warren interpreted that as a 'no' and took the SCD from him. He expertly wrapped a couple of turns of line around the centre of the device, did some clever looping and threading, and then pulled the whole thing tight. The SCD was now dangling from a little cradle of rope at its centre.

"Now get on with it," Warren said, handing the whole thing back to Clipper. "I want his bag and all his personal belongings. Make sure you get any paperwork or computer stuff: disks, memory cards. Don't miss anything."

Clipper nodded and then looked across to Rachel to see how she was doing. She looked like she wanted to say something. Clipper was half expecting her to say 'hurry back' or 'see you in a minute'. Then again, maybe she still wasn't sure he would return. So he said it for her: "I'll be back as quick as I can." She nodded, like she was doing her best to believe him.

"Yeah, yeah," said Warren impatiently and followed Clipper as he made his way to the rear exit steps.

Clipper got as far as: "I'm going to need…" half turning to say it, when Warren handed him a maglite, one of the little ones, about as long as his hand. "Right," Clipper said, taking it from him and turning it on. Then he stepped down to the last rung of the ramp and began lowering the SCD towards the live rail.

He wasn't quite sure what he expected to happen – a loud bang, a spark like a bolt of lightning, maybe the SCD would fly up in the air – but the reality was an anti-climax. He dangled the device, making sure it linked the live rail to the others and still nothing happened.

So he hopped down onto the level of the track and fiddled with the SCD until he had it fitted tightly into place. Then he dragged in a deep breath struggling against a chest that felt far too tight and started walking down the tunnel, away from the train and into the dark.

***

Rachel caught glimpses of Matt's flashlight beam as it bobbed and swung, gradually receding into the gloom of the tunnel. She was sitting on one of the rows of passenger seats just outside the driver's cab. Near her right toe was the bullet hole and splash of blood where Warren had been hit. To the other side of her, in the open space by the double doors, was a broad dark layer of drying blood within which Sebastian had died.

She sat now with her hands in her lap, the nail of one thumb fidgeting against the cuticles of her index finger, her mind fretting just like her hands. Turning her head, she could look over to where her bags lay among the seats, beyond all the blood, just as she'd left them. All ready to go. She tried to imagine for a moment how this nightmare could be sorted out, how she could still find herself on a plane in a few hour's time. The thing was, she could easily picture herself queuing to check in, shuffling those bags forwards a few feet at a time, frustrated that it was taking so long. She could see herself a little later, sitting on hard seats at the gate, among noisy families and sprawled teenagers in headphones, waiting for the announcement to board. Then she'd be on the plane. By midnight, she'd be drowsy and warm, her head propped on a tiny pillow, leaning against her business-class window, watching the faint thread of lights miles below and the occasional flash of moonlight from iced-over lakes. It was easy enough to imagine, and the idea comforted her, but it wasn't real. None of it was going to happen. Right now, it was difficult to believe she was even going to get off this train.

This disaster of a day was not just outside her experience, it was outside of what she had ever expected to experience. She knew bad things happened to people out there in the world, and like anyone who'd ever seen cable news, she'd thought about them happening to her – but not anything like this – not the impossible things she'd seen. They somehow made this ordeal seem... she wanted to say 'unfair'. It wasn't a word she ever used, but there were enough horrors in life you had to prepare for without the world free-associating new nightmares on the spur of the moment. What she'd seen shouldn't have happened.

Nevertheless, here was Warren. Only a few minutes ago he'd trapped the air in her lungs and held her arms pinned to her sides using only – so far as she could see – an angry look. And a few minutes before that she was pretty sure a bullet aimed right at his chest had lost its way and ended up in the ceiling of the train. Warren was a glaring error, a blatant mistake in her understanding of the world.

And yet she'd lived twenty-eight years without encountering anything like him. Her previous life had given no clue to the existence of anyone like Warren. And that left two possibilities. The first was that the world made no sense: it could spontaneously flip into some new mode that ran on different rules, and everything you thought you knew could just slide into chaos. The second possibility was that Warren, and anyone else out there who was like him, were a very tiny part of the world – so tiny that most of humanity went their whole lives without an encounter like this. That was the only explanation that made sense, the only way she could fit this situation into her life while keeping her sanity intact: she was right in the middle of some freak exception to the world's everyday rules. And there was a sparkle of hope in that thought. If Rachel could find her way off this train and onto a plane home there was a very good chance that she would never have to worry about Warren and what he represented ever again. There was no reason she couldn't go at least another twenty-eight years untroubled by the fact of his existence or what it might imply.

Of course, like any good idea, the problems tended to show up once you got down into the details. *If* she could get off this train, her life could go back to normal. But as 'if's went, this one was a bear. Though surely there had to be some chance that once Matt came back with whatever it was that Warren was after, that would be that. And she could almost allow herself to believe that he *would* come back. She was not a trusting soul, but Matt seemed… remarkable somehow, or at least different, though she couldn't put her finger on why she felt like that. Maybe it was just that she didn't know anyone remotely like him. He was an unknown quantity which made it easier to believe that maybe her usual low expectations didn't apply.

Or maybe he *was* a little bit remarkable. At the back of her mind, she was still turning over that strange conversation they'd had, outside, before all this happened. The weird chemistry of that encounter seemed to have left her with an unexpected residue of hope, an unexplained faith that he really was doing his best to help her. Common sense told her it was wishful thinking, but all the same, there it was.

So that would be the first miracle she needed: for Matt to return with Kieran's things. And then what? Warren would get the train moving, they'd finally reach the next station, and Warren would make his escape, leaving her to continue on to Heathrow with just enough time left to check in.

OK, that *obviously* wasn't going to happen. Not with a dead body on the train, another on the tracks and the floor of the train looking like something from an abattoir. But maybe after enough policemen had asked her enough questions, and the delays had stretched out longer than anyone expected, maybe then they'd let her go home. That sounded possible, didn't it? And for that to happen, Warren just needed to release them unharmed.

As it had twenty times already, Rachel's mind's eye dragged her back to the moment the knife went into Sebastian's chest, the gleaming blade slicing down into thick muscle and piercing his heart. There was something particular about the sureness with which Warren had done it. She had known without a doubt when she saw his hands move that he had performed exactly that motion before.

Perhaps the first time he had been nervous, his hands awkward. Perhaps the second time he had been a little steadier, more business-like, but maybe he had still hesitated. But he'd killed Sebastian with a simply, precise efficiency – and no more fuss than if he'd been twisting the top off a jar. So what number had Sebastian been? His third? His fifth?

And she thought back to the look on Warren's face when Sebastian had been shot. It had affected him. He'd been visibly upset. But it hadn't stopped him forcing a knife between his friend's ribs. Once he'd made his mind up, he hadn't wavered – no matter that Sebastian was someone he cared about. So what did that say about Warren? That he was ruthless? That he would do whatever he thought he needed to do? What worried Rachel most was that it suggested – in fact it did more than just suggest – that Warren didn't like leaving loose ends. Matt had said his friend disappeared after working for Warren. Getting rid of loose ends explained that too.

Was Warren going to make an exception this time? Would he leave witnesses behind – especially when he had such extraordinary secrets to protect – secrets that would be picked up by every single newspaper and TV station in the world if they got out?

Sebastian's only crime seemed to be that he might survive long enough to wake up in hospital, where he might say something, or do something, that Warren didn't approve of – or get so delirious with pain or medication that he'd demonstrate one of his impossible abilities to a room full of hospital staff.

Nope. Warren didn't seem like the kind of person who would run the risk of turning on the TV to see her and Matt telling their story on the evening news, followed by an identikit picture of his face filling the screen.

And if he didn't like leaving witnesses behind, was there anything at all she could to protect herself? Like, what if she promised not to talk? Crossed her heart. Really, honest-to-god *swore* that she'd say nothing. And then Warren would have to believe her and he'd be sure to let them both go without hurting them.

Of course he would.

She let her chin drop a little as she felt the hopelessness of the situation. And Warren chose that moment to poke his head round the corner of the doorframe and into the carriage. "Good," he said, seeing her sitting there, looking dejected and defeated. "You just sit tight," he said, and then disappeared back into the rear cab, to keep his vigil for Matt.

She returned to the thread of her thoughts. The endpoint of all that theorising was that she could either sit there waiting to die, or make use of what was probably only a handful of minutes to come up with a plan, a way out, before Warren decided to shut them both up for good. The problem was that her mind was blank. She needed to *think*.

But no ideas came… although… but that was really clutching at straws. A couple of times she'd seen people talking on cellphones on the Underground. She'd never understood how they got a signal, but sometimes people did. Or was that just on tube lines that ran near the surface, where the stations had those huge openings between the platforms where the rain would come in? She couldn't remember. At any rate, she could at least try it. Her cellphone was in her luggage.

Since Warren had just checked up on her, now was the best moment to make a move. She probably had at least a minute before he'd look in on her again. She slipped out of her shoes and padded away from the cab and towards her bag, looking back over her shoulder every few moments for signs that she was being watched. The fact that he'd poked his head around the door kind of implied he didn't have some sixth sense for spying on people. If he looked out and saw her away from her seat she'd say she was going for a Nurofen. I mean, who wouldn't need a Nurofen at this point in the proceedings? Maybe she'd write to them and suggest they used this situation in their commercials.

She edged around the broad pool of Sebastian's blood and reached her garment bag. The phone was in a velcroed pocket up near the handle. Gently, she started to ease the flap up, tearing the fastening apart. But the noise! Dear God, who invented this stuff? No matter how slowly she went, the velcro made a sound like a Geiger counter on full volume – a sound like a Geiger counter sizzling in hot fat. And it was taking too long. Working slowly didn't make the shredding sounds quieter, it just spaced them out. So she tried to arrange the ripping, crackling sound into regular rhythmic bursts so it would sound like the mechanical clicking of some part of the train.

It took more than a minute – probably more like two – before she had the pocket open. She slipped the phone out of its recess and then faced the next problem. She had turned it off before stowing it in her bag. As it powered up it would beep and chirp to let her know it was coming to life. Why did phones have to do that? Was it the same reason that computers in movies had to twitter every time text appeared on their screens? But maybe she could stuff the phone in with her suits and muffle the sound that way. Fortunately the suits were in a section that sealed with a zip – a good quality one that she was fairly certain could be opened silently. She bent down and took hold of the zipper's tab down at the bottom of the bag… and her hand bumped against something cold and solid. Kieran's gun.

Her last glimpse of Kieran had been him holding on to the back of the train with one hand and hugging his briefcase with the other. Before that, he must have either put the gun down or dropped it. Then, as the train's brakes had locked up, the gun must have tumbled forwards in the dark, sliding along the central aisle of the train until it finally encountered an obstacle: her bags.

Rachel was momentarily paralysed. She wanted to grab the gun, but where would she hide it – she was wearing a close-fitting skirt and a tailored blouse – but wouldn't you know it, no holster. And if she grabbed the gun now, would she have the guts to use it? Waving a thing like that at Warren wasn't going to work as a deterrent; he'd made it pretty clear he wasn't afraid of guns. She'd have to wait for a moment when he was distracted, and then she'd have walk up behind him and shoot him. And she wasn't sure she could do that: sneak up, stick a gun in someone's back and blow a hole in him – not even if it saved her life.

She made herself pick up the gun. Wrapping her fingers round the roughened metal grip felt symbolic, like she was agreeing to something before she was really ready. It was like those legal disclaimers that were plastered over every new product these days: by taking hold of this gun you agree to waive your consumer rights to a guilt-free existence; you hereby accept responsibility for the consequences of brandishing loaded firearms in volatile situations; you acknowledge that you may be required to forfeit the remainder of your life or to end the life of another, as specified in your purchase agreement.

She saw that the safety was off, the hammer pulled back. She was fairly sure the slide would be locked back if it was empty. So it probably had at least one round in it. But it must be nearly out of bullets because she could remember at least five shots being fired, maybe more. How many bullets did an automatic hold? She'd fired rifles a few times and watched about a million hours of cop shows. Six shots for a revolver, maybe more for an automatic – that's if the clip had started out full, which maybe it hadn't. At any rate, she wasn't going to be getting into a lengthy shoot-out. If she made her move, she'd probably only get one chance, only need one bullet.

A hissing sound made her jump and her hand tightened reflexively around the trigger, though not enough to fire the weapon, thank god. The sound was coming from all around her. And there was a weird voice, barely audible, horribly garbled coming from all sides. For an insane moment she thought it was… she put the superstitious thought out of her head. What she was hearing was the train's intercom, malfunctioning but still partly working. God, she must be freaked out if her first thought was that she was hearing the voices of the dead.

But there were more immediate priorities than her mental state. Warren would hear the noise and come straight out to investigate. She was standing there with a loaded pistol in her hands in plain view.

The indecipherable voice was trying to make an announcement – she could tell from the intonation – but the intercom was swallowing up the sense of it. Apart from the occasional loud crackle, the rest was just muffled murmurs.

Rachel's instinct was to bury the gun in her bag and retrieve it again later, but what if she never got the chance? She caught sight of her jacket, over by the pool of blood, discarded after Sebastian had died, no longer needed to cushion his head. She flipped the gun's safety catch on, stuffed it into the waistband at the back of her skirt and took four quick steps across to her crumpled jacket just as Warren looked out of the cab and frowned, registering the fact that she wasn't where he wanted her to be.

Making sure to face him, she dipped and came up with the jacket. Holding it up so he could see the reason she'd wandered. She brushed it with her hand, dislodging a few nuggets of broken glass and slipped it on, reaching around to make sure the back covered the grip of the gun.

She gave a little shiver that she hoped didn't look too fake and pulled the jacket's sides around her.

Warren clicked his fingers and pointed to the seat where she'd been sitting earlier, like he was instructing a dog. He was watching her, alert for anything suspicious and this clearly wasn't the right moment to confront him. Obediently she returned to her place, angling her knees towards him as she sat down so as to conceal the bulge at the back of her jacket.

It looked like Warren was about to say something more to her, but a sound from behind him made him turn. Despite his injured foot, he twisted as quickly as a cat to investigate the source of the noise. Then, with a glance back to her, and a finger raised once to indicate that she should stay put, he withdrew into the cab.

Matt must have returned, though she couldn't see him. She could hear him though, and by concentrating she could make out what Warren was saying to him: "Pass it up here. No, you can wait down there. Stay put while I look at this."

Then Warren rejoined Rachel in the passenger compartment carrying Kieran's scuffed leather briefcase in his hands. It was one of the old kind that stood upright and hinged open at the top. It was fuzzy with age, the brown leather faded almost to orange, and now it was streaked with what looked like fluff mixed with axle grease. Warren popped the catch, pulled wide the jaws at its top, and then tipped it upside down, emptying out what was inside. For some reason it made Rachel think of gutting a fish the way the contents spilled out onto the floor of the train. The scene in Jaws, maybe.

Two irregularly-shaped bricks of money hit the floor: half-inch-thick bundles of green notes, piled into thicker blocks and stacked side-by-side, and then bound together with Saran wrap. There were also pens, a phone, a sheaf of papers, some keys and a CD-ROM. Warren flicked quickly through the papers – and Rachel could see the navy and gold of a U.S. passport – before he discarded them and pounced on the shiny silver disk. For a moment he looked triumphant. Then he turned it over and she saw anger tightening his jaw. She wasn't that far from him and surreptitiously tilted her head to read the scrawl across the disk's surface.

In red marker it said, 'J' and then separately, 'Disk 2'. If she'd had to guess, Rachel would have been inclined to think it was the numeral '2' that was bothering Warren, because there was only one disk. He was nodding his head impatiently and repeating 'J' to himself as though trying to remember where it came in the alphabet. Then he pivoted and stalked, stiff-legged, back into the cab. She could just make out the exchange that followed.

"What are you doing now? Get up," Warren barked.

"I thought I saw something. But it was just a bit of glass," Matt was saying.

"Where's the other disk," Warren demanded.

"What other disk?" Matt said. "And what do you mean 'other'?"

"Don't get clever. I can see you're lying," Warren said. "You know something."

Rachel craned her head. By rising up in her seat she could just see Matt's head over the ledge of the train floor. He was still down on the tracks. She looked at him sweat under Warren's gaze. He wasn't doing a very good job of appearing innocent and Warren didn't seem likely to let it pass. Rachel mentally pleaded with Matt to stop looking so guilty and to say something that would reassure Warren.

"Why would I hide something from you?" Matt said at last. "You can search me. And you can look in the tunnel. If there's something I haven't found yet, then maybe it's because he… maybe it's on the body."

"Fine. Search the body. Bring me everything. And I would be particularly delighted if you could find something that looks like this," Warren said, holding up the disk by its edge like a politician waving a manifesto. Then, as an afterthought he said, "And make sure you move the body off the tracks so they can turn the power back on when we're finished with this."

That one moment of confident defiance seemed to have used up Matt's entire supply. She saw him nod slowly and turn back towards the tunnel, his head low. He looked worn out, nervous and pretty much hopeless as well, and her heart went out to him. His job now was to find Kieran's ruined remains and to pick over the body like a grave robber. And when he was done with that awful task, he had to walk back again, probably wondering as he did so whether Warren would kill him when he arrived.

As he trudged off, looking dejected, Rachel found herself wishing he would just leave her behind and run. Whether he came back or not, she no longer really believed it would make much difference to her chances of surviving. He might as well save himself.

But if he was planning to run, wouldn't he have done it by now? The first time he'd got out of Warren's sight he should have made a break for it. But instead he had dragged himself back along that tunnel, carrying the briefcase, heading towards the man who killed his friend.

And there was only one way to explain that. He had come back because Warren had persuaded him that it was the price of her safety – and for some reason, that must have mattered to him. And now he was going to go through it again even though he was plainly scared stiff, even though she could see from his face he dreaded how this might end. If he returned a second time and then Warren cut him down, he would have died because he'd tried to help her. Warren was going to use Matt's desire to protect her to lead him to his death.

She couldn't quite identify the emotion that realisation stirred up inside her, but it burned painfully. It was sickening and strong and she suspected that it was some kind of fury because it made her want to stride into the cab right now and blow Warren's brains out, no matter how suicidal attempting that might be.

But if she tried it now and failed, she would be bringing both of their lives to an end. Better to wait, and choose her moment with a little care. Better to make sure there were no mistakes. She should wait until Warren had his mind on other things – and the best time for that would be when Matt returned again. That would be her chance.

She ran through it in her mind, trying to prepare herself. Warren would be looking down over the track, the light would be coming from behind him so she would need to be careful that her shadow didn't warn him of her approach. On the other hand, she couldn't sneak up slowly. She'd only have a second or two to close the distance between them. And she needed to get close because her best guess was that whatever it was that protected him from harm, it wouldn't work against a bullet fired from a gun pressed into his flesh.

If she'd had to do it right at that second, as she watched Matt drag himself back into the tunnel, she felt sure she could. And so it was agony knowing that she had to wait, that she had to risk letting the fire she was feeling go out. Because then the doubts would crowd back in, her nerve would begin to slip away and soon enough she'd feel cold with fear again.

She was so wrapped up in these thoughts that she twitched with alarm as Warren emerged unexpectedly from the cab. Though it was adrenaline, he would undoubtedly assume it was nervousness.

"I want to…" he said to her, clearly frustrated with whatever he needed to say to her. He tried again, speaking slowly as though telling off a child, "Do you know how I can talk to the driver? I can't make this thing work," he said, pointing back towards the cab.

"I…" she wasn't sure what to say, "I can look."

It was important that he not get behind her where he might see the gun. On the other hand, if they were manoeuvring around each other in a tight space, she might get her chance earlier than expected, which is why she'd offered to help. The difficult part would be to stop him noticing that she was concealing something. When he looked like he might be pausing to let her get by him, she pretended not to notice and rubbed her neck as though it was troubling her, like she'd paused to relieve the stiffness a little.

When she didn't move after a moment, he simply carried on walking and preceded her into the cab. She followed along behind and moved around to the side of him, trying to angle her back to the cab wall which left her tucked in behind the driver's seat. In the gloom, she had to stand uncomfortably close to Sebastian's corpse to do it, but it was the only way to keep the gun hidden.

When she thought about it, she realised that every one of the bullets that had been fired earlier had hit some part of the train. Even the two that had struck flesh had continued on until they encountered metal, glass or plastic. She could even see that one of the windows in the cab had been blown out. It was no wonder that the electronics were malfunctioning. There was a phone set half-way up the frame of the driver's side window and she guessed that would be the intercom. She lifted up the handset and looked at the array of buttons on it. But no matter which one she pressed, nothing happened.

"Great. Thanks for your help," Warren said, unpleasantly. He'd obviously been through this routine.

Then Rachel had an idea. "Listen, there are emergency intercoms all through the train," she pointed towards the compartment they'd just come from. "You can pull the alarm and it will connect you to the driver. We just have to find one that's well away from all the damage."

"OK then," he said, and waited for her to lead the way. Again, she pretended not to notice and held onto the handset as though she was taking one final look at it. He frowned and moved past her and out of the cab, but paused after a couple of steps to check that she was following. She fell in behind him wondering how much longer she could avoid turning her back on him before he noticed that something weird was going on. Then again, if she was frightened of him – which she was – maybe it would seem natural not to want him behind her.

As he turned his back on her and began walking through the train her hand slipped under her jacket and round to the back of her waistband as she wondered whether he was distracted enough to have dropped his guard.

No sooner had she thought it than he stopped suddenly and she nearly walked into the back of him. She snatched her hand away from the gun as he bent over and picked up his discarded boot, and then pulled it back onto his uncovered foot.

Rachel realised that for the last minute or so he hadn't been limping. Had he somehow healed already? She felt a rush of anxiety which brought with it a mental picture of her pumping bullet after bullet into him, unable to slow him down. But, she reminded herself, one stray bullet was all it had taken to put Sebastian permanently out of the picture. You just had to pick your moment carefully.

Warren left his boot laces untied as he walked away from the rear cab and forward through the compartment. He stepped over Rachel's bags and came to a halt next to a red metal handle set high up on one of the carriage's side panels. Rachel ducked into one of the seats opposite so Warren would be free to lead the way whichever direction he set off in.

Warren cleared his throat and pulled the handle down. There were two little red strips on the panel and one of them lit up now, illuminating the words written on it. They said 'Driver Aware'. A moment later, the other one lit up. It said 'Speak To Driver'. And a tinny voice said, "This is the driver. Who is that please?"

Warren gave Rachel a firm look and raised his eyebrows which she could tell meant she was to keep silent. Then he said, "This is Sergeant Chris Hawkins of the Metropolitan Police Counter Terrorism Unit. I have a badly injured colleague here and I need to know if you'll be able to move this train when I give the word."

The driver sounded flustered, "Sergeant, uh, Sergeant Hawkins. Listen, the power's off at the moment and the technical bods are looking into it. We can't go anywhere right now I'm afraid. Can you, er, can you tell me what's going on? You're at the rear of the train, yes?"

Warren said, "I can tell you that my colleague and I attempted to arrest a known terrorist. He turned out to be armed and he fired at my partner, who is now very seriously injured. Then our target jumped from the rear of the train, which I assume is what brought us to a halt. I used the, er, short-circuit device while I retrieved the body. I'm nearly finished now. Then I will remove the device, at which point I need this train ready to proceed to the next station *immediately*."

Rachel could almost hear the driver lick his lips nervously as he said, "A passenger has been killed? Listen, I can't move the train. We'll need to evacuate the remaining passengers and get a crew down onto the track. The investigators have to be informed. That's the rules I'm afraid. My hands are tied."

Warren raised his voice now and spoke with a cold and angry authority. "Now you listen to me. My partner is bleeding all over the floor of this train. He's been shot in the neck and he's dying. The only way to get him medical help in time to save his life is by moving this train. If you let him die you will have me to answer to." Warren paused to let that sink in. "You will be directly responsible for the death of a police officer and that's something which will follow you around for the rest of your days. Think carefully, because you are about to become the most hated man in London." He paused again, for effect. "Now, in a couple of minutes, I will give the word and then you will get the power restored, after which you will do everything humanly possible to get this train to the next station before my partner dies. Do you understand me?"

"I'll see if…" the driver began, tentatively.

Warren's voice was ice as he demanded, "I said, do you understand me?"

"Yes," was all the driver said. And then Warren slid the alarm handle back up cutting off the conversation.

"There," he said to Rachel, turning off the anger in his voice and sounding positively pleased with himself. "That should do it. Now let's hope your boyfriend finds that disk."

But Clipper knew he wasn't going to be finding any disk because he already knew where Kieran had hidden it. Nevertheless, he needed to go through the motions so that Warren would believe he'd run out of options.

Clipper's big idea, the one he had Gary to thank for, was nearly ready to go – all but the last part was taken care of. The problem was that he'd need a full-sized miracle for it to stand any chance of working. And, frankly, Clipper was beginning to have serious doubts that he'd even be alive by the time the opportunity to turn the tables on Warren presented itself. Not only wouldn't he have saved himself or Rachel, but in the meantime, by playing along, he'd have ended up actually helping Gary's killer. That easily made today the worst day of his life and he was still only halfway through listing his problems – because before he could screw up Rachel's rescue and get them both killed, he had to look for a burnt corpse in a railway tunnel and then go through its pockets.

At least he had a pair of latex gloves shoved into the back pocket of his trousers so he wouldn't have to touch the dead flesh with his bare hands. Gary used to buy the gloves from a hairdressing suppliers and they came in handy every now and again for going through swiped bags or luggage that they were planning to ditch. Clipper had always been disappointed that they were looser than medical gloves and never made that satisfying snap like on TV. He pulled on one of them now as his nose told him he must be approaching Kieran's remains.

The body was lying face down and was in one piece. He approached it slowly, trying to ready himself mentally for what he was about to do. The trick, he reckoned, was to narrow his attention down to just the width of a torch beam and not to think about anything else. He did his best to touch nothing, smell nothing and see as little as possible. At least, since he knew the disk wasn't on Kieran's body, he only needed to gather enough personal effects to persuade Warren he'd made a thorough search.

He got through it as fast as he could, and when he was done he had a wallet, a set of car keys, some coins, half a pack of indigestion tablets and a translucent red casino dice. He stuffed them into his own pockets as he found them.

There was only one moment when he thought he might puke, and he managed to get himself under control in time. But it persuaded him that he'd done enough corpse-robbing for one day. He had a plausible haul of personal effects – enough to stop Warren being suspicious – so he turned around and headed for the train. But he walked even more slowly than on the way there, as he tried to think through what came next. He needed to come up with some way out of this situation… and he just couldn't summon any answers. He felt like beating his fists against his skull in frustration.

He might just about have been able to cope with things ending up like this, if it weren't for the knowledge that Rachel was relying on him. He was used to screwing things up, and usually that was nobody's problem but his own. But now, for the first time, he had someone relying on him – and he was going to get her killed. He might even have to watch it happen.

Why couldn't she have picked someone else to rely on? There had to be all sorts of people who'd look at this situation and straightaway get some amazing idea that would sort everything out. But not him. He'd got one extremely long shot in mind that he'd never get a chance to even try. And about the only other thought that had even occurred to him was to sprint flat out to the next station and try to get back before Warren guessed what he was up to and took it out on Rachel. But he knew it was too far, he wasn't fast enough and he wouldn't be able to make anyone listen in time. Maybe someone else could do it, but not him.

So he traipsed slowly back, the light from the train growing brighter and brighter until it dazzled his tunnel-adjusted eyes, until he could make out Warren lurking in the shadows of the rear cab, looking out at him. He even caught a glimpse of Rachel, in the lit passenger compartment, gazing towards the tunnel, but without seeing him. He saw the anxiety on her face and it felt like she was accusing him, blaming him for letting her down. *Sorry Rachel*, he said to her, soundlessly. *You just picked the wrong person to depend on.*

As he came close to the base of the train's escape ramp, Warren stepped out of his corner and called out to him, "Did you find it?"

He didn't reply straight away. This being bad news, he didn't want to shout it. He wanted to be close enough to say it quietly. When he'd closed the gap he said, "There wasn't any disk." He was standing to one side of the ramp now, while Warren stood on its top step and looked down at him. He didn't look pleased.

"Did you check the track on the far side of the body? Did you make sure you didn't walk past it?" Warren demanded.

"I was very careful," Clipper lied. "There was no disk." Clipper unloaded what he had found, reaching up to place each item on the floor of the rear cab.

Warren leant down and snatched up the pile, glanced quickly through the wallet before swearing. And then swearing again. He tossed Kieran's effects into the light of the compartment behind him. Clipper waited patiently, knowing that they couldn't be very far from the end of things now. Warren would rant and curse and then he would think about his next step… and then his attention would come back to Clipper and what to do about him. And, unless Clipper was very lucky, that would be that – for him at least. Then, soon after, the same thing would happen to the girl in the next compartment who'd made him smile and who had no one else but him to help her.

"Can I come up?" he said at last, thinking it couldn't hurt to ask.

"Oh, I don't think so," Warren said, sounding far from pleasant.

That was pretty much what Clipper had expected. He stood there, waiting to see if there'd be any more instructions. He'd known he wouldn't make it back into the bright comfort of the passenger compartment again. He expected to die down there on the tracks, filthy and afraid.

"You know, I think I've finally figured out where I know you from," Warren said.

Clipper thought for a moment and then laughed. They were the words he'd been afraid of hearing since he'd first set eyes on Warren today. But now it was too late; Warren's little feat of memory could hardly make things any worse, could it?

"You were friends with Gary Wilson, weren't you?" Warren asked.

Hearing Gary's name on Warren's lips offended Clipper; Warren shouldn't be allowed to say that name. "And you killed him, didn't you?" Clipper said, angry, and figuring there was no point in concealing it.

Warren smiled and spread his hands. "He was too much of a thinker. I told him to stop, but he couldn't help himself. He was always putting two and two together. Sooner or later that causes problems." Warren looked down at Clipper and said, "What I really should have done was pick you instead."

Insults too? Great, thought Clipper. He didn't know how to reply. Perhaps there was nothing left to say. He stood waiting for whatever came next.

"Get that contraption disconnected," Warren said, nodding towards the short-circuit device, "and I think that will do it for you."

Clipper took a breath and turned around. He bent over and wrestled the metal clamp loose from the rail. Then he picked it up by its rope and carried it over to where Warren was pointing, before setting it down on the bottom step of ramp.

"Yup," Warren said. "I think you're probably finished now."

Here it comes, thought Clipper, and the feeling hit him a moment later. A tightness settled on him, pressing into his chest, his neck, his face – and with a jolt of panic he realised he couldn't move air in or out of his lungs. Warren might as well have taped a bag over his face: he couldn't breathe. And now his body was starting to react. He could feel the veins in his neck standing out and the thud of his heart growing heavier and more violent until each beat was like being thumped in the chest.

He was looking up at Warren who had a slight frown on his face – but it wasn't concern – he was simply concentrating. Clipper doubted that he was even the most pressing thing in Warren's mind at that moment. Clipper was a chore that needed finishing, that was all. Warren's thoughts would be on other things, like getting away, or what he was going to tell his bosses about all this.

Very quickly things were starting to get hazy for Clipper and his thoughts were scattering as fast as he could chase them. As he did his best to keep Warren's face in focus, he wondered whether his killer was even now thinking about how he was going to dispose of Rachel. Half delirious with oxygen starvation he found that thought still had the power to make him sad.

Clipper was starting to lose the edges of his vision now and his thoughts were scarcely more than a jumble, but it almost looked as though Rachel was there, pressing up against Warren in a way that Clipper's confused brain found unsettling. It was like she was hugging herself to him and Clipper hated that thought. He'd been hoping that she liked him instead.

But now he was dying and she was getting cosy with his killer. He'd expected better from her.

But a moment later there was a sound like an explosion, muffled somewhat by the invisible barrier that was wrapped around Clipper's head, and then Warren was toppling forwards. Simultaneously, cold air burst into Clipper's lungs and it was like the lights came back on in his brain; everything around him became sharp and hard-edged, and he could think again.

Rachel was crouching over Warren, who had fallen to his knees. She had the gun pressed to the back of his head and angled up slightly so that the grip of the weapon was pressed into the fabric of Warren's backpack.

Down on the tracks, Clipper was on all fours, gasping for air, but he was looking up, trying to take in the scene. Warren was down too, and doubled over, but he wasn't dead. He groaned loudly and tried to rise. Rachel pushed the gun's barrel hard into the base of his skull and said, "I can fire this thing before you can stop me. So don't move until I tell you to."

Then she looked over at him and said, "Matt? Are you OK?"

He was still hyperventilating, but he could talk. "I'm OK," he said. "What do you want me to do?"

She said, "The driver's ready to move the train. So let's get the power turned on and get going. Can you take care of the short-circuit thing and get this door closed?"

"Yeah, no problem," Clipper said. "And, er… thanks very much." It sounded a bit stupid, saying 'thank you' for saving his life, but if that didn't warrant a 'thank you', then what did? Plus, Clipper wondered if he might not be just a tiny bit high from the combination of adrenaline and lack of oxygen.

Rachel was talking to her captive. "Stand up slowly. Turn *very* slowly. And then walk back to that intercom. Tiny steps all the way."

Warren managed to get to his feet with a bit of trouble. Clipper couldn't see exactly where he'd been hit, but he had his hands clamped over his chest high up on his right side. There was a strange wheezy noise as he breathed that Clipper could hear from down on the track. He looked pretty messed up, and yet he was able to stand.

Clipper reckoned that even with another hole in him, Warren would still be about as dangerous as a tiger on crystal meth, but watching Rachel, how sure she sounded, he was starting to believe that she and him had a chance of making it to the next station alive. As Warren turned and Rachel kept herself tucked in behind him, he was starting to feel a surge of hope. His stupid plan to take Warren out wouldn't be needed now, and thank god for that.

And then he saw something that made his breath stick in his throat all over again. Rachel pushed the gun into Warren's neck, urging him to start shuffling forwards and Clipper caught sight of it as it passed into the light that streamed through the open doorway. The slide was back, covering the hammer. The gun was empty.

If Warren suspected, if he decided to try his luck, they were finished.

As Clipper grabbed hold of one of the steel cables and pulled himself up onto the ramp, he thought of all the things that could go wrong in the few minutes it would take them to get to the next station and he wondered what he could do to help Rachel. Hopefully she'd just get Warren to lay down on his front as soon as they were clear of the rear cab, but he didn't want to risk suggesting it in case it gave Warren ideas.

At any rate, Clipper needed to get the track clear and the door closed as quickly as possible. So he grabbed the SCD off the bottom step of the ramp and poked it in through the busted window of the cab. Then he withdrew into the cab and tried to figure out how to get the steps folded up and the door hoisted back into position. A few seconds of trial and error and he had it slammed shut.

Picking up the SCD and holding it like a rather ungainly baseball bat he moved towards the doorway, praying that Rachel still had Warren under control and he didn't need to go hand to hand with him. That would be a short fight.

Rachel had got Warren most of the way down the carriage and now he stood, dripping blood and wheezing painfully, in front of the emergency alarm. Rachel was right behind him, the empty gun pressed into his back, the barrel tucked into the hollow at the top of his spine.

"Tell him," she said. And when Warren didn't respond, but just stood, slightly stooped, arms clamped across his injured chest, she repeated it, this time screaming it at the top of her voice, "Tell him to move this train or I'll kill you and do it myself."

Warren reached up, slowly and painfully, the motion putting a strain on his wounded flesh. Then he pulled the handle down and waited for something to happen.

A moment later there was a crackle. "Driver here," the voice over the intercom said.

"Everything's ready. Let's get moving," Warren said, his voice sounding hoarse and uneven. Then he folded the alarm handle back in place. A moment later he began to choke, doubling over, just as the normal compartment lights came on. They looked dazzlingly bright after the relative gloom. The noise of compressors filled the carriage, making the floor vibrate. It felt like the train was coming back to life.

"Stop moving," Rachel commanded, as Warren shuddered with each cough. "Just lay down on the floor."

Good, thought Clipper. *Get him to lie down and stay there.*

Clipper saw Warren get his choking under control and begin to straighten his back. He set one knee on the ground, ready to lie down. And then Clipper saw Warren's head turn a little and pause. Clipper followed his gaze and realised what had happened: he was looking at Rachel's reflection in the window, lit up by the full glare of the compartment's lights.

And Clipper knew what would happen next. There wasn't even time to shout a warning. Warren had seen the condition of the gun. He twisted around and caught Rachel across the jaw with his elbow, slamming her to the ground. Then he stood up carefully, swaying on his feet. He straightened up very cautiously as though wondering whether his wound was as bad as he'd been making out. Then he took his hand away from the wound and inspected the damage. Rachel was still at his feet, momentarily dazed by the blow and not yet able to find her feet. The empty gun lay on the floor nearby, discarded now.

Warren touched the oozing hole in his chest carefully and gasped. "You people," he said, sounding disgusted. Then he looked Rachel in the eyes and said, "This next part, you're not going to enjoy."

Clipper knew what to do. He couldn't wait any longer. The timing would just have to take care of itself. Before Warren could do anything, Clipper shouted out his name. Warren looked round to see what he wanted.

"I know where the other disk is," Clipper called out. He'd seen Kieran's hand fidgeting, seen the little knife cutting into the upholstery while Warren went to attend to his fallen comrade. And Clipper had seen the glint of the disk as Kieran slid it inside the hole he'd made. Now Clipper moved to that spot, halfway along the row of seats nearest the rear cab.

Warren was still directing his attention at Clipper; he hadn't turned back to Rachel yet. Clipper rested the unwieldy metal SCD on the floor, propping it up against the seat, and nearly tripping over the trailing rope in the process. Then he plunged his hand into the slit in the seat cover.

He pulled out the disk and held it up. "See?" he said. He looked at it himself and read aloud, "J. Disk one. E-mails, plans and accounts. That has to be what you were after. Whatever he stole, whoever he was working for, I bet it's all on here."

"Give me that," Warren said, that curious bloody gurgle evident in his voice. Then he started walking towards Clipper. "*Now!*" he yelled.

Clipper scuttled backwards to the door of the rear cab, wedged the disk in the doorframe and applied some pressure. "Stop right there or I'll break it," he commanded.

Warren stopped. For a moment. Then he began to edge slowly forwards. "Let's do a deal," he said. It was just like before, when Kieran had stood on more or less this spot and Warren had offered him a deal too. Clipper wondered if this reckless feeling inside him was what Kieran had felt too.

Warren was using that same old reasonable voice again: "Matt? You know I can track you down if I have to. Now that I know you were Gary's friend I can find out everything else about you. But that's good. Because it means right now I can let you go. If you cause trouble for me, you know I'll be able to hunt you down. But if you don't… then we're fine. You understand? So if you give me the disk now, I won't have to take it off you. You live, and I get the information I came for."

The curious wobble Clipper could hear in Warren's voice didn't seem to be emotional – the man was as sure of himself as ever; it was something to do with his injury. Clipper realised that Warren was trying to make a deal even as blood trickled into his lungs.

Then, with a lurch the train moved, and everyone grabbed for something to hold on to. A second later, the brakes slapped into place, the train shuddered to a halt and the compressors kicked in again.

"We'll be out of here in a minute," Warren said. "I bet you could probably be home in an hour. But if you break that disk, I'll kill you, and that will be that."

"And what about her?" Clipper asked, nodding towards Rachel.

"Of course. You can both go," Warren said. Clipper waited for him to argue, to explain his conditions and lay out the terms of the deal, but he just repeated, "You can both go if you let me have that disk."

Maybe if Warren had asked for Rachel's surname, demanded to see some proof of her identity, Clipper might have been tempted to believe him. But he didn't. And that meant Warren had no intention of letting her leave the train alive. Which pretty much settled it in Clipper's mind. Any doubts he'd had about what he was planning to do were gone.

Again the compressor cut out and again the train lurched, but this time the motion continued and the train began to move forwards at last.

As they pulled away, Warren was beginning to sound a little pressured. "OK, we've run out of time, so let me turn this around and see if that helps," he said. "I'm going to come over there and kill you now. See if you can talk me out of it." Then he started towards Clipper, his eyes hard and fixed on his target. His hands were clamped so tightly over the hole in his chest that his fingers were white and the steps he took were slightly unsteady, but there was no mistaking his murderous determination.

"Right. OK," Clipper called out in a tone of surrender. He held up the disk. "OK." Then he leant over and set it on the floor, in the doorway to the rear cab, before clambering up onto the nearest seat, as though he was trying to get out of Clipper's way.

The train was accelerating now, the driver obviously having taken Warren's words to heart, and Warren was moving faster too. Clipper tried to get past him by hopping across the seats, stepping rapidly over the arm rests as Warren dragged himself down the aisle towards the disk. But as they passed, Warren threw out his hand, cracking Clipper across the side of the head with a solid punch and sending him sprawling headlong into the aisle.

Warren reached the doorway to the rear cab as, behind him, Clipper tried to get up. He'd smacked his head pretty hard and the fall had been awkward. His arm had been trapped under him as he fell. He thought it might be broken, which would explain why he couldn't seem to get it to work.

Rachel rushed forwards to help him and Clipper screamed at her to get back. He sounded so desperate for her to listen to him that she stopped dead.

Warren had the disk now and was tucking it into a pocket in the leg of his trousers. With the hole in his chest slowing him down, it took him a few seconds. By the time he was finished, Clipper had managed to crawl away as far as the double-doors – all of five metres forward from where Warren was standing. He was almost at the exact spot where Sebastian had died.

The train was really moving now, a fact Warren was obviously very aware of as he said, "I think we'd better make this quick." Then he threw out his hand with a stabbing movement, thrusting it towards Clipper. It was just like the punch that Warren had thrown in the club, the one that never landed. But this time it was Clipper who felt the awful impact of it. It felt like a bomb had gone off inside him. His chest was lit up with pain as though he'd stepped out in front of a bus. Or maybe, as some part of Clipper's reeling brain insisted on suggesting, as though he'd been hit with the force of a train.

And at that moment it happened. There was a sound from the rear cab as the rope snapped taut. Clipper had wrapped a loop of it around the driver's seat, to hold it until the last second. With a crack like a whip, it snatched itself free. Then the metre-long metal bar of the SCD leapt backwards and flew through the door of the cab, encountering Warren as it did so. As the clamp struck him, the train was doing just under forty miles an hour and the rope, tethered as it was to a spot just under where the cab had previously stood, transmitted all of that velocity to the steel shaft of the SCD.

Clipper wasn't able to stay conscious long enough to see it hit. But he heard the incredible noise it made and knew it had happened. He knew Rachel was safe. He just wished he'd been able to see Gary one last time and explain that he'd solved the riddle of the perfect iPod lift. The trick was that you swapped it around. Always choose a train over a platform. You put *yourself* on the receding train with the prize and you left the cord behind, along with your unlucky victim. Gary probably wouldn't have approved of modifying it so he could kill someone, but he'd have been pleased that Clipper had solved the riddle, and even more pleased that he'd used it to save a life. It's just a shame it hadn't been Clipper's own.

His last thought was that maybe he was about to get a chance to see Gary in person and thank him for giving Clipper a way to keep Rachel alive.

***

Rachel sat in the kitchen looking out across the fields of home – perfectly familiar, but made new with a fresh fall of snow. She had coffee in her cupped hands. Her mother had made it at around six, before she went out to check on the horses. Rachel had slept in until after seven. The house had been warm and deserted, except for a sleeping dog toasting itself on the base of the cooking range. He looked up at her, whined politely, and then laid his head back down.

She tucked her feet in their thick socks beneath her and sat at the counter, half focusing on a distant pair of crows, arguing over something they'd found in the snow, while the other half of her mind was miles away.

She'd waited a fortnight before leaving the UK. There'd been questions to answer, even more than she'd expected. And it had been made a little trickier by her need to bend the truth in a couple of areas and to leave out anything that no one would believe anyway. Fortunately, it was fairly clear to the police that she was just a passenger who got caught up in something terrible. With the way things were, you didn't accuse US citizens of anything unless the State Department said you could. And you didn't inconvenience the employees of US banks, even once they'd resigned, unless you had no choice.

So Rachel turned Warren's death into an accident. Or rather, she said that she couldn't explain it and the police concluded for themselves that the trailing rope had snagged on something, all by itself. Any knots Matt had tied were gone. The fake cops, whoever they had been, must just have been careless. And the back of the train was sufficiently wrecked to make the exact sequence of events a matter fit only for theories and best guesses.

In Rachel's version, she and Matt had watched as the fake cops and an unidentified gunman fought. Both of the fake policemen had been shot. Had she seen a knife? She wasn't sure; she'd been hiding. And then the gunman had thrown himself from the train. So far so good. Then she and Matt had both been injured as the train slammed to a halt, which explained her bruises. With the train stationary, the least-injured fake cop had needed a hand retrieving the gunman's body and Matt had agreed to help, but he was unsteady on his feet and had slipped, falling from the back of the train onto the rails. The fake cop got Matt back on board, and decided to forget about the body on the tracks. He wanted to save his companion, who was in a bad way, by getting the train moving again. Shortly afterwards, the rope had snagged, a terrible accident had occurred, and that was that.

One or two problems arose when the forensics report suggested that her sequence of events didn't match the evidence, but no one knew what to make of that – and when Rachel could offer no explanation, there wasn't much anyone could do about it. Two crooks, posing as policemen, had cornered a third man and driven him to kill himself. No one could implicate her in any of it and Matt was in no position to contribute anything to the enquiry. The police had even retrieved a single fat brick of US dollars, which seemed sufficient motive for the violent squabble. The gun, when it was eventually located, shed no light on anything. It had been wiped clean of fingerprints.

So Rachel had returned home, later than expected, but more glad than ever to be leaving London behind. There'd been just one last piece of business for her to take care of before she departed. She'd gone to visit Matt in hospital and told him everything she'd done, what she'd said and what her plans were. And then she'd flown home to find that her mother – who'd been following the British news – was even more grateful to have her daughter home safe than Rachel had thought possible.

In fact these last three weeks had been a wonderful dream she didn't want to wake up from. Her mother and her hadn't quarrelled. There had been a few tears at first, but very little had been said, and now they had both settled into a comfortable peace. Rachel didn't know if it would last, but there was every reason to think it would be put to the test later that very day. Rachel was expecting a visitor.

Matt phased in and out of consciousness for a long while. The warm cotton-wool of painkillers kept him from understanding the few glimpses of reality he gulped down, before he sunk back into his concussed and medicated stupor.

It was a week before he had any control over the comings and goings of his mind, before he had any say in when his eyelids dropped closed. And it was ten days before they let him have a visitor. The first person they let in to see him was his girlfriend. Matt knew she'd only called herself that so that they would allow her in, but he liked the idea of it all the same.

Rachel looked gorgeous, although the puffy, yellowing bruise across her cheek hurt him worse than the ache in his ribs when he saw it. He wanted to get up, make a fuss of her, even just manage to sit upright, but he couldn't. After a moment he stopped trying.

Once the nurse had left, she looked him over, concern in her eyes. "Does it hurt?" she asked.

"Only when I'm awake," he said. He smiled at her. "Thanks for coming to see me. I was hoping you would."

She looked horrified. "Are you kidding? Of course I'd come and see you. You saved my life. And look at what it cost you." She took in the cast on his arm, the drips, and the contraption holding his splintered ribs together. "You don't do things the easy way, do you?"

Matt was worried that he was going to laugh for a second, which didn't bear thinking about. He'd probably fall to bits if he tried it. "Well, some of it is a bit vague," he said. "But I remember nearly dying and then I remember you being there and I could breathe again."

They said nothing for a moment, their eyes wandering, occasionally connecting, and then one of them would glance away.

"I've got something to tell you," Rachel said at last.

Matt said nothing. She went on, "I hid half of that money. It took them ages to come and get us. So I just grabbed it. The police didn't search my bag. A friend of mine is looking after it, though he doesn't know what's inside the case I left him. Here's the key." She pulled a little slip of metal out of the pocket of her jeans and laid it on top of his bedside cabinet.

"Why..." Matt said, looking confused. "Why are you giving it to me?"

"Well, you said..." Rachel sounded awkward. "You said you were unhappy. You said you were," she dropped her voice, "a thief and you didn't want to be. There's about a hundred thousand dollars there. It won't make you rich, but it might let you start over."

Matt didn't know what to say. Rachel added quietly, "It's enough for a plane ticket too. When you're feeling better."

"You want me to... You're inviting me to visit?" he said.

"You can visit," she said. In little more than a whisper she added, "Maybe, if you like it, you could stay?"

Matt's face was burning now. He wanted this more than anything, but he couldn't let himself believe it. This wasn't how real life worked. He needed to tell her the truth before she found out anyway.

"I want to," he said. "I think it's the best offer I've heard in my whole life. But, what about the fact... I mean we don't really know each other. You don't really know me, is the point. Someone like you..." he was struggling now, finding the words getting stuck in his throat. "I would just make a fool of myself and you'd be disappointed."

Rachel leaned over and kissed him carefully, once, on the lips.

"You've got a point," she said, "I don't know very much about you. And I don't think we've got much in common. It takes years before you really know someone. All I know about you is that you make me laugh – sometimes. And that I can absolutely trust you with my life." She smiled at him and gently took hold of his hand. "And I've noticed that you can't seem to take your eyes off me. I decided that was enough to be going on with."

"Well, if you put it like that," Matt said haltingly, but with a smile on his face. "We should probably at least *try*. Shouldn't we?"

Rachel was beaming at him. "Yeah, because if I set my standards any higher I don't think there'd be anyone in the world who qualifies."

They sat for a little while, not saying much, but both OK with that. And then Rachel explained to Matt the story she'd told the police. When she was done, he said, "You think they believed it?"

"I think they're used to things not making sense. They just don't have any better theories," she replied.

Rachel looked thoughtful for a moment and then pulled something flat and shiny from the back pocket of her jeans.

"Listen, Matt," she said. "The things we saw – the things that Warren could do – they were pretty weird, right?"

He nodded. And she went on, "As well as taking half the cash, I also had a quick look in that guy Kieran's wallet. I found this." She placed the metal rectangle, about the size of a business card, next to the key.

"I don't know why he carried it with him, but I've got a theory. I think it was to remind him that there were more important things in life then understanding people like Warren. I know it's not easy to walk away from a mystery, but I think this one time that you should. Tell me that you won't try to find out more about who Warren was. Just get better and then fly out to see me, OK?"

Then she leaned over and kissed him again, and said goodbye.

It was another three weeks before he could get out of bed and even then his doctors advised him against it, but his bones were knitting and he wasn't in any danger. He'd had thirty-one days to mend and it was enough that he could get around if he had to. The day after he got out of the hospital he picked up the money Rachel had left for him – and the day after that he booked a plane ticket to Seattle.

He slept through most of the flight and then they made him ride in a wheelchair from the gate. Rachel was waiting for him when a helpful Skycap wheeled him into the arrivals area.

He thought about the metal card she'd left for him as she drove them past white fields under a sky so pale and clean he could hardly believe he was on the same planet as London. He looked over at Rachel now. The bruise was gone from her cheek and she looked well and happy and beautiful. When she turned to smile at him, he thought his heart would burst with the feeling of it. He didn't think he could ever say it aloud, he wasn't brave enough, but all he wanted in the world was a chance to make her happy. If he never did anything else right in his life that was OK, if he could do that single thing.

After she'd left his hospital room he'd reached over and picked up the metal card. It had been a struggle to get his arm all the way over there and as he moved it, he found she'd left a picture too. It was an old photo of her, holding a horse's bridle and smiling. She had written 'see you soon' on it.

He read the words on the metal card: 'why study power when you can study happiness instead?' She needn't have worried. He didn't need to be told twice. He pushed the card so that it slipped off the edge of the table and into the bin. Then he propped the picture against a water glass, so that he could see it when he turned his head, and he settled back to think about the future.

The End

The events of *Underlife* take place before those of *Adept* and *Ex Machina*. In the subsequent novels different central characters take up the story.

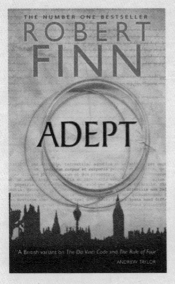

ISBN: 978-0954575-91-5

ISBN: 978-1905005-06-2

> Read exclusive extra material
> Win copies
> Get great deals
> Find out more...

about *Adept* and *Ex Machina*,
Robert Finn's bestselling sequels to *Underlife*,

at

Snowbooks.com/RobertFinn

Underlife © 2008 Robert Finn
ISBN 9781905005697
Proudly published by Snowbooks Ltd
120 Pentonville Road | London | N1 9JN
Small Publisher of the Year 2006
www.snowbooks.com
All rights reserved
Printed by J. H. Haynes & Co. Ltd., Sparkford